D1580628

Michael Scott was born in Dublin in 1959.

He has written three volumes of Irish Folk and Fairy Tales for adults, edited HALL'S IRELAND: MR & MRS HALL'S TOUR OF 1840 and also written a full-length novel, A CELTIC ODYSSEY, all published by Sphere Books.

Michael Scott is married and has a daughter and son.

Tales from the Land of Erin: Volume 1
A Bright Enchantment

MICHAEL SCOTT

SPHERE BOOKS LIMITED
London and Sydney

First published in Great Britain by
Sphere Books Ltd 1985
30 32 Gray's Inn Road, London WC1X 8JL
Copyright ‹ 1985 by Michael Scott

Illustrations by Carolyn Scrace

The manuscript of this work was prepared on an ICL PC15
computer, using Word Star software, courtesy of POS Systems
and Fred Hanna (Booksellers) Ltd, Dublin.

**TRADE
MARK**

Set in Century

Printed and bound in Great Britain by
Collins, Glasgow

for Courtney,
a first edition.

CONTENTS

Tales from the Land
of Erin: Volume 1
A Bright Enchantment

CHAPTER ONE

The Arrival Of The Tuatha De Danann In Erin: The Stowaway

The land of Erin was invaded many times in the past, and amongst the greatest of its invaders were the Tuatha De Danann, who were called the People of the Goddess. They were powerful magicians and they brought to the island many, many gifts, including the arts of healing, writing and metal-working.

However, how they discovered Erin is a strange tale, for they found it almost by accident...

The ship was made of solid gold.

Daire stood on the dockside and stared up at the beautiful vessel. It was twice as long as any ship he had ever seen before – long and slender, high at both ends and with a sail that shimmered in the early morning sun like silk. It was a truly magical craft.

All the inhabitants of the city of Murias were talking about the ship – which was to be called the Seeker – and the voyage it was preparing to make. There were rumours that the four tribes of the

Tuatha De Danann would soon be sailing to a new land. But the Seeker would go first and find that new land for the People of the Goddess.

Of course, everyone wanted to be on that ship, but only the best had been chosen. They had come from the four magical cities of Finias, Gorias, Falias and from Murias itself. The bravest warriors, the finest magicians, sorcerers and physicians, the best carpenters and metal-workers would be going. Even the king and his court would be sailing on the Seeker. Once a suitable land had been found, they would set about making it ready for the rest of their race.

Daire had been standing on the dock since sunrise. He was a young boy of about ten years old, with a mop of thick black hair and sharp black-coloured eyes in a thin, almost pointed face. He had stood watching the men come and go, the food and weapons being loaded and the famous people who would sometimes appear on deck. He had even seen Diancecht, the doctor and magician who had discovered the art of healing and curing, who had arrived in his carriage of polished black metal, which was drawn by two snow-white unicorns.

The young boy stood back as a troop of soldiers in their silver armour marched down to the dock and up the ramp to the ship. They wore the crest of the Black Crow, the sign of Morrigan, one of the great women warriors of the De Danann people.

Oh, how he wished he were going. But he was only the son of a blacksmith, although his father always claimed that the family were related to Goibniu, the famous blacksmith, who had actually discovered how to work and shape metal. There was no chance of a blacksmith's son going on the great adventure.

The morning wore on, and the blazing sun made

the water sparkle like jewels and a heat haze
shimmered over the surface of the waves. Daire
remained on the dockside. He had found a little spot
between two huge bundles of rope, where he was
sheltered from the heat of the day and which was
close enough to the ship so that he could watch the
people coming and going.

In the early part of the afternoon, when most of
the city of Murias was resting, Nuada, the King of
the Tuatha De Danann, and Oghma, his brother,
who had discovered the art of writing, visited the
ship. They did so quietly and without fuss, but
Daire, from his hiding place, could see them clearly.

Nuada, the king, was a huge man, one of the
tallest men of their race. His hair was black – so
black that it shone almost purple in the sunlight
and he wore a simple silver band around it instead
of a crown. He wore plain silver armour with a sun-
wheel design on the breastplate, and there was a tall
battle-axe strapped to his back.

'When do we sail?' His voice was deep and carried
clearly across the waves to the young boy.

Oghma, the king's brother, shook his head. 'Soon,
very soon now. Perhaps even later on today.'
Oghma was smaller than his older brother, and
slimmer, and his hair was already beginning to
turn grey.

'Today,' Nuada said slowly. 'We must be away not
later than today. We have a long journey ahead of
us.' He paused and then added, 'and we haven't
much time left.' He lifted his head and looked up
over the town, towards the mountains.

Daire squirmed around in his hiding place and
followed the direction in which the king was
looking. But all he could see was the huge volcano
which was called Lord Thunder. He heard the king

3

speak again and turned back.

'Who knows when the Lord Thunder will speak again?'

His brother nodded. 'The priests and magicians say it will be soon.'

'And then?' Nuada asked.

'They say it will destroy the Isle of the Goddess,' Oghma said slowly, nervously running his fingers through his thin hair. 'They say it will bury the four cities beneath a covering of lava many miles deep.'

Nuada sighed. He slapped his brother on the shoulder and turned away, but his voice drifted across the waves. 'All the more reason for us to find this new land for our people.'

So, Daire thought excitedly, it was true. When the Seeker had discovered the new land and made it safe, then the rest of the Tuatha De Danann would join them. He looked back over his shoulder at Lord Thunder and felt his heart beginning to pound. But would they be in time before the mountain spoke and threw fire and lava down onto the cities? Even as he watched a thin wisp of dark smoke drifted up from the cone into the clear blue sky.

Daire crouched back in the shadows as the king, his brother and their advisers hurried from the ship and set off in their chariots, back in the direction of the palace. Soon the ship grew quiet and the guards, now that the king had left, became more relaxed. They drifted off to one side and huddled down on the deck, out of sight, and then Daire heard the rattle of dice off the metal decks.

The young boy slipped from his hiding place and darted towards a pile of heavy wooden boxes. From there it was only a step to the water's edge. He sat down on the dockside, and hesitated for a moment, while his heart pounded painfully in his chest. This was his last chance to get aboard the Seeker. The idea had come to him suddenly; it was a mad, crazy, foolish idea, and he knew if he thought about it for too long, he would be too frightened to act. So he didn't think. He took a deep breath and slipped down into the waves.

The water was warm and salty, and Daire's head bobbed to the surface almost immediately. He was only a few feet away from the ship, and its huge anchor chain hung down almost by his head. But this side was closest to the guards. Daire took a deep breath and then, bending his body almost double, he dived down and under the ship.

He came up on the seaward side. He was red-faced and gasping and he clung to one of the links of the anchor chain while he caught his breath. He could see the huge sweep of the bay of Murias, with its white-washed villas and red-bricked houses lining the beaches. Higher up on the mountains that almost completely surrounded the city were the palaces of gold and silver, copper and bronze of the Lords of the Tuatha De Danann. In the early morning and late evening when the sun was low in the sky, they glowed and shimmered and the tiny diamonds set into the walls sparkled like a thousand stars. It was a very beautiful sight.

But then he swung around and looked up at the blackened sides of Lord Thunder the volcano, and he shivered to think that all this would soon be gone, buried beneath the thick lava.

Daire took a deep breath and began to climb up the huge links of the anchor chain. The chain itself was almost as thick as his own body and he found it easy to climb up along the links.

He peered over the edge of the craft. Off to the right-hand side – the starboard side, as it is called on

a ship – the guards were still playing dice, and too busy to notice him. Still clinging to the edge of the deck he looked around for a hiding place.

There were a lot of large wooden boxes piled not far from him. Some were open and seemed to be packed with long bolts of cloth. Closer still there were sacks of fruit and vegetables, and beside them cases of salted meat. Daire's stomach rumbled and he realised how hungry he was. He hadn't eaten since morning.

The boy waited until crewmen were actually rolling the dice before he heaved himself up onto the deck and rolled quickly across to the boxes and sacks. He squirmed beneath a sack of apples and wedged himself in between two boxes of fruit. The smell of the apples was almost overpowering and he took one and rubbed it on his sleeve before biting down deeply into it. It crunched so loudly that he stopped chewing in fright in case he had been heard. But then he heard the dice rattle on the deck and knew it was safe.

Daire settled back against the rough sacking to finish off his apple. No one would be looking for him, he knew. His parents, who lived outside the city, had apprenticed him to one of his father's brothers who was a magician. They thought that if he managed to learn some minor spells he would be able to help them around their small farm and forge. However, his uncle, although a very kind and cheerful man, was also very forgetful. It was one of the reasons he was not a very good magician – he kept forgetting half his spells. Daire smiled to himself, his uncle probably wouldn't even notice he was missing.

His stomach rumbled again, and he reached for another apple...

Daire awoke suddenly. He was cold and shivering and he felt a little sick. For a moment, he didn't know where he was, but then he suddenly remembered and realised that he must have fallen asleep.

There were people moving around him, and voices calling and talking together. Daire squeezed in tighter into his little hiding place – and then he noticed that the ship was actually moving. For a single instant he was frightened, but then he smiled widely. His great adventure was under way.

He heard footsteps approaching.

'Right then, let's start moving the fruit and vegetables.' The voice was gruff and sounded slightly breathless. 'We'll shift them down there.'

And before Daire had a chance to move, the sack of apples that he was hiding behind was pulled away and he was caught in the torchlight.

'What's this?' the gruff voice roared. 'A stowaway?'

A huge hairy hand reached in for Daire, but the young boy managed to slip from under it and dart out between the man's legs... only to run straight into another man. A hand clamped down on his shoulder holding him tight.

'What's going on here, eh?' The second voice was softer and gentler, and Daire thought it sounded familiar.

'A stowaway, sire.'

Sire, Daire thought. But only kings were called *sire*... He looked up into the face of Nuada, King of the Tuatha De Danann. 'Sire,' he whispered and attempted to bow, but the king was still holding onto his shoulder.

'Are you indeed a stowaway?' Nuada asked him gently.

Daire could only nod.

'Why?'

The boy looked up into the king's hard grey eyes. Like most of the Tuatha De Danann race, they were slightly slanted, and looked huge in his long, thin face.

'Why?' the king asked again.

Daire shrugged uncomfortably. 'I wanted to come with you,' he said. 'That's all.' He paused and then added, 'Have we come far, sire?'

'Too far to return,' the king said. 'Will your parents not be worried?'

'I am apprenticed to a magician with a very bad memory,' Daire said. 'They won't even know I've gone, and I don't think he will either.'

Nuada nodded slowly. 'Well, we're stuck with you now. But what are we to do with you?'

'I have some skill in metal-working and my father is related to Goibniu the Blacksmith...'

Nuada smiled. 'Ah. Well then, I think you shall be the Smith's apprentice.' He looked over Daire's shoulder. 'Laeg, see this lad is fed, and then bring him to the Smith.' He turned back to Daire. 'This may be a long voyage; I'm sure I shall see you again.' He nodded and turned away. The young boy and the crewman both bowed deeply.

Laeg straightened up and looked down at Daire. He saw a young boy of about ten years old, with thick black hair and sharp, bright eyes. He was wearing a none too clean tunic that was held around the middle by a broad leather belt. 'I suppose the first thing to do is to get you fed,' Laeg said kindly. He was a huge bear of a man with copper-coloured skin, a head of bright red frizzled hair and a beard to

9

match. He was not of the De Danann people, Daire realised, but was one of the Fir Dearg, the Red Men, from the forests that lay to the west of the Four Cities.

'I am a little hungry,' Daire said. 'All I've had is a few...'

'Apples,' Laeg smiled. He ran his thumb across the boy's sticky chin. 'I can see that. And when we have you fed,' he added, 'we'd better get you washed up. We can't have you meeting the famous Goibniu with a dirty face, now, can we?'

Daire nodded uncertainly. 'What's he like?' he asked, following Laeg as he made his way towards the kitchen, or the galley, as it was called on a ship.

The Red Man looked over his shoulder and smiled. 'Och, but he's a terrible man, a terrible man altogether.'

Daire met Goibniu later that evening. The Smith had been given the huge space below deck for his tools and equipment, and when Laeg led Daire down below, the young boy's first impression was of a huge cave with walls of metal. It was badly lit too, with only a few glowing bowls of light scattered here and there, sparkling off the gold walls, and sending dancing shadows across the mysterious bundles that were piled everywhere. In a far distant corner someone was whistling tunelessly and tapping a long bar of metal gently.

Laeg nodded. 'That's Goibniu. I'll leave you here – and remember, don't let him bully you.'

'I won't.'

The Red Man nodded. 'I'll wait for you above.'

Daire approached the pool of light cautiously. He was beginning to get a little frightened now – he had heard such terrible tales about the famous man who had discovered metal and how it could be heated, shaped and twisted into everything from a pot to a sword to a ship. Goibniu – what a strange name, Daire thought, even for the De Danann, but then the Smith wasn't a true De Danann. His mother was from the People of the Goddess, but his father was one of the Fir Dearg. Daire tried to walk on his toes, his footsteps sounding very loud on the metal decks.

The gentle hammering stopped.

Daire stopped also, feeling his heart beginning to pound.

'I don't want an apprentice!' The voice was rough, like two stones rubbing together, and Daire jumped with fright.

'Do you hear me? I don't want an apprentice. You'll drop things and lose things and probably burn yourself – or me, for that matter. So you can go away!'

'I won't drop things,' Daire said, angry at the man he couldn't see yet. 'My father is a smith – and a good one too, probably as good as you – and I've never dropped anything on him; nor have I ever lost anything, and I've certainly never burned anyone.'

'Yes ... well.' There was a cough. 'I still don't want an apprentice.'

'Nuada said I was to be your apprentice!' Daire said, coming a few steps closer.

'Nuada knows nothing about working metal,' Goibniu snapped.

'But I do,' Daire said.

'Do you? Do you really?' the Smith asked. 'Come here then.'

The boy walked into the circle of light. He gasped with surprise when he saw the Smith. Goibniu was only a little taller than himself, but he was broad, with huge bulging muscles beneath his reddish-coloured skin. However, his hair was black, and his eyes were slightly slanted, and both his ears and chin came to a point. His eyes were green, and very, very bright.

The Smith pointed to the workbench before him. His thumb was almost as thick as Daire's wrist. 'Tell me what that is.' He nudged a bar of metal with his finger.

Daire picked it up and turned to the light. It was the colour of butter and was silky smooth to the touch. He ran his fingernail along it. 'It's gold,' he said.

Goibniu said nothing, and just pointed to another piece. 'And that?'

'That's silver,' the boy said without hesitation.

'And that?' Goibniu nodded to a third piece.

Dare looked closely at it. In the reddish light from the oil lamps it was difficult to make out its true colour. 'It looks like silver,' he said at last, 'but I'm not sure.'

'You're wrong,' Goibniu said quietly, picking up the smooth bar. 'It's called white gold.'

'Oh. Does that mean you won't take me?' Daire asked.

Goibniu shrugged his huge shoulders. 'Well, you did know the other two...' he began.

'And my father is your cousin... or perhaps a second cousin,' the boy added.

'Well then, in that case you're almost a relative,' the Smith said. 'You can be my apprentice.' He smiled broadly, and Daire noticed that one of his teeth was made of gold.

'When do I start?'

'Right now,' Goibniu said. 'There's a pile of new swords over there that need polishing, and when you've finished that, you can fill up the oil lamps and check the fire.' He paused and then added, 'What's your name, boy. I don't think we were ever properly introduced.'

'My name is Daire.'

'Daire,' the Smith nodded. 'And you can call me Goibniu, or Master.'

'Yes Master Goibniu.'

The Smith smiled hugely again. 'I think we'll get along fine,' he said.

The Seeker continued to sail south for seven days and seven nights. When the wind died down, the Lords of the Tuatha De Danann would gather and call up a magic wind, which would push them on.

However, on the seventh day a storm wind began to blow. Dark, heavy clouds gathered on the horizon, and flurries of rain and sleet rattled across the metallic decks, and some of the more experienced sailors promised that the coming storm would be a terrible one.

The crew hurried about tying everything down, and Goibniu had Daire replace all the loose bars of metal back into their heavy wooden boxes, and lock up all the tools so that they wouldn't be thrown about when the storm finally broke. The Smith then left the young boy while he went to a meeting with the rest of the De Danann lords.

Daire had just about finished tidying up when the Smith returned. The small man was red-faced and excited. 'We must clear a space in the centre of the floor,' he said breathlessly. 'All the Lords are going to work a piece of High Magic.'

'What's High Magic?' Daire asked.

'The oldest kind. The magic that came into this world when the world was made. It is the most powerful. Now, hurry, hurry, we must clear a space. They'll be here soon.'

'I'll get some help,' Daire said, and quickly ran up the ladder onto the deck.

'There you are! I haven't seen you for a while, young man.'

Daire recognised the gruff voice and spun around. 'Laeg!' he said with a smile.

The Red Man smiled. He nodded below decks. 'How's he treating you?'

'Oh, he's good to me.'

'You're not letting him bully you, are you?'

Daire smiled. 'I don't think he could if he tried; he's too kind-hearted. But Laeg,' he said, 'you must help me. The Lords will be gathering shortly to work some High Magic, and we need some help to clear the floor below.'

The Red Man nodded. 'I'll help you.'

Between them, they soon had the deck clear, and just as they were finishing, Goibniu returned with a tall, black-haired, sharp-faced woman. She glanced at Laeg and Daire, but ignored them.

'Who was that?' Daire whispered.

'That is Morrigan, the Warrior. You've seen her soldiers about the deck surely?'

'Their crest is a black crow on a white circle?'

Laeg nodded. 'That's them.' He nodded in the direction Morrigan and Goibniu had gone. 'Be careful of her, she's a very dangerous woman. And now, I'd better go; the rest of the Lords will soon be here.'

'Should I go?' Daire asked.

The Red Man considered. 'No. You're the Smith's apprentice. You should stay here, in case he wants you – but stay out of sight until you're called.'

'Thank you Laeg, for all the help,' Daire said.

The Red Man smiled and nodded. He then turned and hurried up the ladder onto the deck, while Daire found himself a spot in amongst the boxes where he was safely out of the way, but close enough if his Master wanted him.

Soon, the De Danann lords began to arrive. Nuada arrived first, his silver armour shining red in the light of the many oil lamps. His brother Oghma arrived shortly afterwards, followed by old Diancecht, the famous magician and physician who had discovered the art of healing. Brigit came in with him. She too was a great healer and the finest poet in the Land of the De Danann.

Then two women moved quietly down the steps, and Morrigan moved out of the shadows to join them. The three women were very alike, as if they were sisters. There was Badb, the Lady of Battle, a tall white-haired, pale faced woman, who wore plain black armour, and beside her stood Macha, who was sometimes called the Raven, because she was so dark.

The last to arrive was Manannan. He was not truly of the De Danann people but was said to be the last of an older race, and was sometimes called the Lord of the Sea. His hair and beard had a greenish tinge and even his skin was slightly greenish. His eyes, like those of a fish, never blinked. He was also able to breathe under water and was said to be able to raise up storms, and control the winds.

When everyone had arrived, they gathered in the centre of the room in a rough circle. Nuada stepped into the circle, and raised his hands for silence.

'I thank you all for coming,' he began. 'I have asked you here so that we can join together and work some of the Old High Magic. My lord Manannan tells me that the storm that is fast approaching is very powerful, and that even with our magic defences it will still damage us beyond repair.'

'What do you wish to do, brother?' Oghma asked quietly.

Nuada smiled, his eyes flashing brightly in the light of the torches. 'I wish to raise this craft above the storm!'

'Above the storm?' Goibniu rumbled. 'What do you mean.'

The king raised his arm and pointed upwards. 'We're going to fly!'

The king stepped back out of the circle, and then he joined hands with Oghma and Diancecht who stood on either side of him. They in turn joined hands with the persons standing beside them and soon all the lords of the Tuatha De Danann were joined together.

Daire, watching intently from his hiding place, saw them all bow their heads and then they began to sing in their own secret language. He saw the oil lamps begin to flicker and then dim, and soon he could barely make out their shapes in the darkness.

Suddenly the voices stopped. Daire shivered. He felt cold and the air tasted damp. He looked around, but he could see nothing. But when he looked back at the circle of the De Danann, he saw that they were each outlined in a glowing circle of dull blue-green light. They began to chant again and slowly, the light began to spin and revolve around the circle, growing brighter all the time.

And then it began to move upwards.

Daire felt the Seeker tremble and then it too moved – as if it had been pulled up and out of the water. Slowly, very slowly, the glowing circle of light moved up around the bodies of the lords, and as it moved higher, so too did Daire have the feeling that the ship was also moving upwards. When the blue circle of light had reached head-level it stopped and so too did the feeling of movement.

The De Danann lords stopped their singing and chanting and then, without saying a word, the circle broke up and they filed out one by one, until only Goibniu was left alone. He looked very tired and old, Daire thought as he slowly straightened up and stepped out of his hiding place.

The Smith looked up. For a moment he looked angry, but then he smiled. 'Don't let the others know that you saw what happened,' he said quietly.

'I thought you might need me,' Daire said.

Goibniu nodded. 'You can blow out the lamps,' he said. 'I'm tired now, I'm going to rest for a while. Magic is very exhausting.'

'Have we really moved upwards?' Daire asked. 'Are we really flying?'

The Smith shrugged. 'I suppose we are. We're probably flying above the storm clouds. When the storm is over then we'll go down to the sea again.'

Morning came and Daire went about his usual duties of feeding the animals and cleaning out their cages. It wasn't really his job; Laeg was supposed to do it, but the boy had offered because he loved animals. He shivered in the thick fog that covered the ship. It was cold and damp and so dense that it was difficult to see anything that was more than an arm's length away. He had attempted to look over the side to see if they were actually flying, but he could see nothing in the fog.

It stayed like that all day. And the next day and the next day and the next, and so on for over a week with no sign of a change. On the morning of the eighth day, Daire was once again looking after the animals and birds when he heard voices in the fog quite close to him. He recognised the voices as belonging to the king and his brother.

'I cannot understand it,' Nuada said, 'we should be near land, and yet we've no way of telling.'

'Can we not use some magic to help us?' Oghma asked.

'Manannan has warned me against using any sort of magic. He says the land we are nearing is inhabited by demons who are able to smell magic. We don't want to warn them.'

'Then how are we going to find the land?'

The king and his brother loomed up out of the shadows before Daire. 'I don't know,' Nuada said, and then he spotted the boy. 'Hello. I knew we would see one another again.'

Daire bowed deeply to the two De Danann lords. Nuada and Oghma bowed slightly and were about to move on when Daire looked up into their faces. 'My lords ... ?' he said slowly, and then he stopped.

Nuada knelt down on the deck beside him. 'Yes ... Daire, isn't it?'

'Yes, my lord.'

'What were you about to say?' Nuada asked.

'My lord, if we cannot find the land ourselves, why can we not let something else find it for us?' Daire said excitedly.

The king shook his head. 'I'm not sure what you mean.'

'You said that we were close to the land?'

'Very close indeed.'

'Well, my lord, there is a hive of bees here,' Daire began. He saw the king beginning to frown and hurried on. 'What if we were to let them go – and then follow them. Don't you see? – they would head straight for the nearest grass and flowers.'

Nuada looked over his shoulder at his brother. 'What do you think?'

Oghma nodded slowly. 'I think it might just work,' he said. 'Yes, I think it might just work.'

Nuada straightened up suddenly. 'We'll try it now. Gather the De Danann here. And you,' he turned to Daire, 'prepare that hive of bees.'

The lords of the Tuatha De Danann gathered quickly, and the crew of the Seeker slipped away from their duties and climbed up into the slack rigging to look down on what was happening. They were all tense and curious, wondering why the king had called them together so early in the day.

Nuada raised his hands for silence. The fog gathered on his silver armour in tiny beads which shimmered and shook as he moved. 'This won't take long,' he said loudly, but the fog muffled his voice and those at the back had to strain to make out what he was saying.

'This is Daire,' he said. 'Most of you will remember he is the stowaway we found the day we set sail. He has been the Smith's apprentice since then, and Goibniu tells me he is an excellent pupil. However,' he continued, 'we think he may have discovered a quick way to bring us to our new land.' He stepped back and laid his hand on Daire's shoulder. 'Tell them what you told me,' he said softly.

'*Me!*' the boy whispered loudly.

'Yes, you,' the king smiled. 'It was your idea.' He urged Daire forward gently.

The boy bowed briefly to the De Danann lords. His great idea suddenly didn't seem so good now with all those stern faces and hard eyes staring at him, but then he caught sight of Laeg's red hair and beard at the back of the crowd. The Red Man nodded at him and then winked. Suddenly Daire felt much better.

'My idea,' he said loudly, but he coughed and had to start again. Someone in the crowd laughed. 'My idea,' he continued, 'is to release the swarm of bees we have on board with us. Their senses are much more sensitive than ours and they will be sure to head straight for the nearest grass and flowers. All we have to do is to follow them,' he finished in a rush.

There was a moment's silence and then someone in the crowd began to clap. Soon everyone, including the lords and ladies of the De Danann were clapping.

Diancecht the physician stepped forward. He looked at the boy with his sharp, piercing eyes. 'It is a brilliant idea,' he said in his quiet way. 'Simple, but brilliant.' He looked closely at Daire. 'If you ever get tired of being the Smith's apprentice you can always become mine,' he added. The physician then looked at Nuada. 'When do we try this excellent idea?'

The king shrugged. 'How about right now?' he said.

Diancecht nodded. 'Right now it is then.'

The crewmen scurried to their places, while the De Danann lords took up their positions below deck, so that they could work their High Magic and bring the craft down. Only Morrigan the warrior-woman remained on deck beside Daire, because she had the sharpest eyesight and would be able to follow the flight of the bees.

When all was in readiness, Daire took hold of the big wicker basket and stepped forward into the prow of the Seeker. He could feel his heart pounding against the wood of the basket as he set it down on the golden deck. He then took a deep breath and slowly and carefully eased the top off.

For a moment nothing happened, and then a loud and angry buzzing came from inside. The buzzing grew louder and louder until even the wood was vibrating and then, in one solid mass, like a thick cloud, the swarm of bees took off. They spun around over Daire's head for a few moments, and he didn't even breathe, nor was he stung, and then they shot out over the prow of the Seeker and down into the fog.

Morrigan darted forward and leaned out so far over the rail that Daire was afraid she might fall out. She called aloud in the secret language he had heard them use before, and the ship tilted downwards slightly, and increased speed. Again and again, Morrigan shouted directions, sometimes bringing the Seeker down, sometimes a little to the left or right as the swarm of bees changed direction.

And suddenly it was all over.

Morrigan shouted aloud in surprise as the Seeker broke through the clouds and they found that they were hovering just above a smooth and grassy plain. To one side the sea crashed onto a rocky beach and, on the other, low hills rose into mountains. The land seemed green and fertile and stretched as far as the eye could see.

And the grassy plain was dotted with flowers on which the bees were feeding happily.

Nuada came up and laid his hand on Daire's shoulder. 'Well, what are you going to call this place? It was your idea after all.'

Daire looked down over the side of the Seeker at the huge green plain covered with flowers. 'I would like to call it the Plain of Honey,' he said softly.

Nuada nodded. 'Then that's what we'll do, but we'll use the old language of the De Danann, and call it *Mag Mell*.' He turned to the crew and the De Danann lords. 'This will be the new home for our people. Let's cheer its discoverer...'

And that is how the People of the Goddess, the magical Tuatha De Danann, came to the Land of Erin.

CHAPTER TWO

The Departure Of The Tuatha De Danann: The Secret Places

The Tuatha De Danann ruled the land of Erin wisely and well for many, many years, and they used their great gifts for good. But in the end new invaders came from the south. These were the Milesians, and they brought with them a terrible weapon – iron.

The De Danann people were defeated at the great battle of Tailltiu, for their magic could not overcome the iron swords and spears of the newcomers.

And so the Tuatha De Danann departed from the World of Men and went to their Secret Places...

'We are now the last of our race in this land,' the old man said slowly, looking around him at the deserted village. In the grey light of the dawn, with the morning mist still clinging to the stones, the round houses looked very lonely.

'But we're not really leaving,' his son said quickly.

Faolan, the old man, shook his head sadly. 'We were once kings in this land – and now we are nothing.' He picked up his long staff and stepped out into the deserted street. Donn, his son, took one last look back at his home, and then followed him.

They moved slowly and sadly down the street to the stream where the rest of the village had gathered with their goods and belongings. There were only a few people there, not more than twenty. Many had gone to fight in the war with the Milesians, but only a few had returned.

Faolan, the village elder, raised his hand for silence. He was an old, old man now, his hair and beard snow-white and his face creased with lines. He had come to Erin on the Seeker, the ship which had carried the first of the People of the Goddess to this place.

'You all know why we are here,' he said very softly, although, in the quiet of the morning, his voice carried clearly. 'The armies of our people have been defeated, and many of our leaders are dead. As you know, we must leave this world.'

'But our homeland is destroyed,' one of the villagers said. 'The Four Cities are now lost beneath the waves.'

Faolan nodded. 'We are leaving this world – but we are not leaving Erin,' he said quietly.

'I don't understand,' the same villager said.

Donn stepped forward. 'What my father means,' he said quickly, 'is that the Lords of the De Danann have prepared new homelands for us – "Secret Places" they are called. They have prepared huge caves under the ground for us to live in. These will be called forts and they are magical; they have their own light and heat and we will be able to grow whatever we will need.'

'Also,' his father added, 'we will never grow old there. We will be immortal.'

'So, you see,' Donn said, 'although we are leaving this world, we are not truly leaving Erin. We will continue to live on beneath the ground in our forts.'

'But will we be able to return to this world?' someone asked.

Faolan nodded. 'These forts will look like rounded hills from above, but there will be a door in these hills, and, on certain evenings, we will be able to ride out into the World of Men again.'

The villagers murmured amongst themselves for a while and then one stepped out of the crowd. He was a small, dark-skinned man, looking more like one of the Fir Dearg than one of the De Danann. 'And what happens if someone doesn't want to go into this fort?' he asked.

'No one is forcing you, Lugh,' Foalan said. 'If you go there and find you do not like it, you will be free to leave.'

'I don't think I want to go and live underground,' Lugh said, almost to himself. He shifted his hammer on his shoulder, and rubbed his other hand on his thick blacksmith's apron.

'But you'll have to go into hiding then,' Donn said. 'You cannot allow yourself to be caught by any man.'

'I won't be caught,' Lugh said confidently, 'and sure, even if I am, I can always escape'

Faolan shook his head sadly. 'I'm sorry you're not coming with us, Lugh. We'll all miss you. However,' he added, 'you won't be alone, because there are people in some of the other villages like you who do not wish to live underground. Surprisingly, a lot of them – like you – are either blacksmiths or have some Fir Dearg blood in them. Perhaps you could all join together.'

Lugh nodded. 'Aye, perhaps we could.'

'But a word of warning,' Faolan said. 'Be careful not to hide all your wealth in one place in case you are caught. Spread it around in a dozen different places. Try and travel only at night, and wear clothes that will blend in with the trees and grass or the flowers if it is summer.'

The small man nodded. 'Thank you for your advice. I will remember it.'

Faolan smiled. 'And we will remember you when we need something mended.' The old man then turned back to the rest of the villagers. 'We must go now.' He raised his arm and pointed into the sky towards the east. 'Look, the sun is rising. Take a good look at it – it is the last sunrise you will ever see.'

The Tuatha De Danann then mounted their tall, thin horses, with the children on smaller ponies and, with Donn in the lead, they set off at a gallop into the west. Faolan was the last to leave. He sat on his horse and looked around and there were tears in his eyes. Then he nodded to Lugh and turned his horse into the west.

The small dark man watched the Tuatha De Danann ride from this world. Soon they would become a myth, he knew. What he didn't know was that soon he, and the others like him who had not gone with the De Danann, would also become legend. For they would later be called Leprechauns.

CHAPTER THREE

The King's Secret

This is a strange tale which has two different endings. It is about a famous king of Ireland who was called Labhra Loingse. He had once been known as Labhra the Dumb King, because he swallowed a fieldmouse in his beer one day and was struck dumb. However, some time later he was struck a terrible blow on the back during a fight, and he coughed up the mouse – which was still alive – and he found he could talk again.

However, Labhra Loingse was unusual in another way; he had a very strange secret...

The king sat under the shade of an old oak tree and dangled his feet in the water. It was a very warm day and he was hot, sticky and tired. He had stripped off most of his heavy armour, wrapped it up in a bundle in his cloak and tied it to the saddle of his horse, and now he only wore a light shirt and breeches – and his heavy horned helmet.

Even on the hottest day, Labhra Loingse never removed his helmet. No one knew why, and if anyone ever did find out, the king had them killed. For he had a dark and terrible secret: he had the tall, hairy ears of a horse. An old fairy woman had

cursed him with them one day when he was still a young man because she had found him beating his poor horse who couldn't run any faster. She had suddenly appeared in front of him, standing beside a stone, and his horse had reared up in fright, throwing him backwards, leaving him shaken and dazed on the ground. He had looked up to find the small, grey-haired, grey-eyed, grey-clad woman staring down at him.

'You are a cruel man, Labhra Loingse,' she had said coldly.

'But it's only a horse,' Labhra had protested.

'Only a horse? Only a horse?' The old woman had smiled then, and her smile was hard and bitter. 'I do not have much power left, but I do have enough magic left to do this!' She closed her left hand into a fist and then pointed the first and little fingers at him. The king felt his head tingle and buzz and then his ears began to burn. He clapped his hands to his head – but instead of covering his own small, rounded ears, he felt the tall, thin shapes of a horse's ears. And when he looked up, the old fairy woman had gone.

The king visited many of the magicians and doctors in the land, but no one could remove the spell. They said that it was fairy magic – the oldest and most powerful magic in the world. Now this was a time ago when both men and women wore their hair long, and Labhra Loingse allowed his to grow until it covered his horse's ears. And he always wore a horned helmet with two holes cut on the inside of the helmet, so that the tips of his ears could stick up inside the horns.

However, twice a year the king would have his hair cut, because if it grew too long people would begin to wonder what he was hiding. The barber

31

always came from one of the furthest parts of Erin, and when he had cut the king's hair – and seen his ears – the king would have him killed before he could tell anyone what his secret was.

One Midsummer's Eve, the king sent his guards across his kingdom to find a barber to cut his hair. Of course, by this time there were very few barbers left in Erin and the few that remained went into hiding about this time of year in case they should be chosen to cut the king's hair. And so, the only barber they could find was a young man who worked in a tiny village in the south-west corner of Erin.

Now this young man was the only son of a widow and when the king's soldiers took him away, she travelled to Tara, where Labhra had his court, and she begged the king to spare the life of her son.

The king didn't want to, but at last he agreed, only on condition however that the young man would keep a secret for the rest of his life. The woman swore that her son would never betray the king's confidence. The young man – whose name was Marcan – was then brought in and, when everyone had left the room, the king took off his helmet and ordered the barber to cut his hair.

Marcan had only made a few cuts when the tops of the ears appeared. He stopped cutting and carefully parted the hair, revealing the king's ears.

Labhra swivelled around in his chair and stared up at the barber. 'So now you know my secret – and you should die because you know it. But your mother has been here and she has made me swear not to kill you because you are her only son and all she has left in this world.' The king paused and then continued. 'She also said that you would keep a secret, and so I will not kill you – on the condition

that you swear an oath here and now never to tell anyone what you have seen this day. Well?'

'I swear it,' Marcan said quickly. 'I will tell no living man.'

The king nodded. 'Good. Now, you may continue cutting my hair – and I will appoint you the royal barber. Twice a year you will come to the palace and cut my hair – but remember your promise...'

'I will never forget,' Marcan swore.

Because Marcan had not been killed by the king and because he had been appointed the Royal Barber, most people assumed it was because he was the best in the land, and he soon became a wealthy man and had to move to Tara where he would cut the hair of all the lords and ladies of the court.

Of course, people would often ask him why the king wore that strange horned helmet or why he had always killed the barbers before him, but Marcan would shake his head and say he didn't know. But people didn't believe him and kept pestering him for the answer.

Soon Marcan became very depressed. He felt that if he didn't tell the secret to someone he would burst. So he went to one of the holy men of the time, a druid, and he asked him for advice. The druid asked him to repeat the oath he had sworn to the king, and Marcan said, 'I swore I would tell no living man.'

The druid then threw back his head and laughed. 'Why then, all you have to do is to go out and tell your secret to the first thing you meet, be it bird or beast, bush or tree. Your problems will then be solved.'

Marcan thanked the druid and hurried out beyond Tara's walls and stopped at the first tree he came to. He stopped and looked around and after making sure no one was near he leaned close to the

34

bark of the tree and whispered softly, 'Labhra Loingse has horse's ears; Labhra Loingse has horse's ears.' And now, having told something his secret, Marcan went home happy and relieved and the secret never again troubled him.

However, some months later, some woodmen came along and cut down that tree and they sent it off to one of the greatest craftsman in Erin at that time and he, in turn, made it into a harp for Craftne the Harper.

There was to be a great feast in Tara that night, and Craftne had composed a new song in celebration of the king. The great hall was silent as the harper approached. He was a small, richly dressed, fussy man and he carried his harp in a specially made leather bag slung over his shoulder.

Craftne bowed to the king and then to the assembled lords and ladies. He sat down on a low three-legged stool and slowly removed the cover from his harp. It was a beautiful instrument, tall and slim, and with tiny precious stones set into the richly polished wood. Craftne ran his long fingers down the golden strings and a delicate shivery sound drifted out over the hall. He touched the strings again and then swept his hand from one end of it to the other. The sounds it made should have been lovely – but instead, in a high-pitched squeaky voice, it shouted, 'Labhra Loingse has horse's ears... Labhra Loingse has horse's ears... Labhra Loingse has horse's ears...'

Craftne dropped the harp in fright and it shattered into pieces. The king stood up so suddenly that his horned helmet fell off and, because he had just had his hair cut, his ears were exposed for all to see. The king made a grab for his helmet, but he slipped on the steps to his throne and fell to the ground and broke his neck. The strange thing was that when he died his ears turned back to normal, so everyone knew that he had been cursed by the fairies for some evil deed.

There is another ending to this tale. When Marcan whispered his secret to the tree, he was overheard by two magpies who were perched on the branches above his head. When he had gone, they flew off in two different directions and there they met two more magpies.

'Labhra Loingse has horse's ears,' they said, and then the four magpies flew off north, south, west and east, and soon they met two magpies each.

'Labhra Loingse has horse's ears,' they said, and then they all flew off in different directions. By morning all the birds of the air knew the king's secret.

Labhra Loingse woke early the following morning. He got out of bed and went to the window to watch the sun rise over his kingdom. A magpie came and perched on the windowsill and looked at the king with its hard bright eyes.

'Labhra Loingse has horse's ears,' the bird said, and the king was so shocked, both at hearing the bird speak and because it knew his secret, that he died of fright on the spot.

CHAPTER FOUR
The Crow Goddess

When St Patrick brought the Christian faith to Erin, the old Celtic gods disappeared, and men soon forgot about them. But the old gods did not die – because they are immortal and cannot die. They are still around, and sometimes they reappear...

The sudden shower of rain sent Dermot running down the hill towards the cave for shelter. He should have brought his heavy oilskin with him. His grandfather, who always knew what weather was coming, had warned him that it would rain before evening, but Dermot, standing by the door of his house, had just laughed and run out into the sunshine.

As usual, his grandfather had been right. Shortly after midday, when he had been sitting down to his lunch of bread and milk, he had seen the first of the grey clouds appear on top of the mountains. But it didn't start to rain until it was almost time to head for home. The sky suddenly darkened – and then it poured down.

Dermot dashed into the cave just as the first heavy drops of water spattered onto the ground outside. He was a short, stout boy, ten years old, with a wide, smiling face and hair that was always falling into his eyes. He sat with his chin resting on his knees and watched the rain churn the earth outside the cave into mud. Further on down the hill, he saw the sheep moving into the shelter of stones and behind some of the small, stunted bushes. The boy sighed; it looked like the rain would come down for a while. Well, he would sit it out for an hour or so, but if it showed no sign of easing up he would have to make a run for home.

But the rain, instead of lessening, seemed to become even heavier. It drummed off the ground and stones, and the wind, which had also grown stronger, now and then sent flurries of icy rain into the cave mouth. Very shortly, a gale was blowing, and now leaves, twigs, pieces of branches and even small stones were being tossed past the cave mouth by the wind.

Dermot shivered. It had grown cold, and he was only wearing short trousers and a light woollen jumper. He couldn't leave now – he would be soaked in seconds and would probably catch a terrible cold. He kept moving further back into the cave, but now he had his back against the cold stone wall, and he couldn't go any further. However, he knew that if he didn't appear at home for supper then his father or older brother would be sure to come looking for him.

There was a sudden gust of wind which whipped dust and dirt into the cave and then something small and black was thrown into one corner. For a moment Dermot thought it was just a leaf but then he saw that it was moving feebly. He crept closer to have a look. It was a bird; a small, bedraggled crow.

Dermot took the bird into the palm of his hand. It couldn't have been more than a few days old. It was soaking wet and some of its feathers were ruffled

and some were missing. It must have been caught in the open by the storm and tossed on the wind. He turned it over carefully in his hand, checking for any cuts or signs of broken bones. Luckily, there didn't seem to be any blood and he was able to stretch its wings and rub its thin legs without any difficulty.

'What are we going to do with you then?' he asked softly, rubbing his fingers down its back. The crow's hard black eyes watched him carefully, and its beak slowly opened and closed.

'I'm not going to hurt you,' he said. He crept back to the rear of the cave and huddled in close to the wall. In the distance thunder rumbled and the dark sky was brightened almost immediately by distant lightning.

The bird seemed to shiver in his hand and Dermot suddenly realised how cold it was. He turned up the end of his jumper and carefully wrapped the small bird in it, and then held it close to his chest.

Thunder and lightning boomed and flashed again, closer this time, and he felt the bird's tiny body twitch with fright. 'Sssh, sssh now,' he said. It was only a very young bird, and it occurred to him that it might never have heard thunder before.

As the late afternoon wore on into evening and the storm showed no sign of lessening, Dermot began to get very worried. What was going to happen if the storm continued on into the night? His father or brother would not be able to go out and look for him - and even if they could, they might walk right outside the cave and he wouldn't even see them. Besides, he didn't think the bird would last through the night without some food and heat.

He began to cry, very, very softly to himself.

He might have fallen asleep – he wasn't sure. He did remember resting his head on his knees and closing his eyes, and at that time it had been dusty grey outside. When he raised his head from his knees it was totally black.

And then he blinked and blinked again, for he suddenly realised that he could see – even though it was night outside! The light was very dim, and was slightly greenish, but he could clearly make out the walls of the cave, and the little lichens and rock plants that clung to the stone, and he could even see his own grubby knees. The bird! He reached for the tiny crow – but it had gone.

'Do not worry yourself, the winged-one is safe!'

The voice came out of nowhere and seemed to echo inside his head. It sounded like that of a woman. 'Do not be frightened, human, I will not harm you.'

Dermot looked around, but he could see no one. 'Who…who are you?' he whispered, his voice sounding strained and cracked. 'Where are you?'

The air in front of the cave mouth seemed to shimmer, as if he were looking at it through a heat-haze, and then he found he could make out the shape of a woman. The image was blurry and indistinct. He bit his lip and said nothing.

'I am Morrigan,' the image said, and it suddenly hardened, and he found he was facing a tall, thin-faced woman wearing ancient-looking black leather armour and holding a tall battle-axe.

Dermot squeezed his eyes shut, thinking the image would go away when he opened them again, but when he did she was still there. He looked closely at her thin face, high cheekbones and slanting eyes, and he thought he could make out pointed ears beneath her thick black hair, and then

41

he recognised her as one of the *Sidhe*, the fairy folk.

'What...what do you want?' he managed to whisper.

The terrifying woman smiled, and her dark eyes lit up as if from within. 'I have come to help you,' she said.

'To help me?'

Morrigan nodded. 'I am – I was – the Goddess of War and Battles when the Tuatha De Danann ruled this land. But when the Sons of Mil came, we knew that our time was done and we left this world. And then the faith of the Christians was brought to this island by the small Roman, Patrick, and people no longer worshipped the old gods and we faded away. But we live still,' she added suddenly. 'I had another name,' Morrigan continued. She held out her hand and in it the small black crow nestled comfortably, looking plump and healthy. 'I was called the Crow Goddess.'

Dermot blinked. He had heard his grandfather tell some of the ancient legends about the terrible Crow Goddess. He felt his throat tighten. 'You said you wanted to help me...'

Morrigan nodded. 'You helped one of my creatures, so too will I help you. Close your eyes,' she commanded.

Dermot squeezed his eyes shut. There was a rushing sound, like wind, and then he suddenly felt warmer and he realised that the sound had changed. When he opened his eyes he found he was in the barn behind his own house...

Dermot's family did not want to believe him when he told them about the Crow Goddess. But there was no other way that he could have been suddenly

43

transported from the cold cave nearly five miles away to his own home except by magic, now was there? .

CHAPTER FIVE

The Fairies' Revenge

The fairy folk are a strange people. They can be nice and kind one day, and then mean and spiteful the next. If you are good to them, they will give you anything you desire, and yet, if you anger one of them, they can make things miserable for you. But if you do happen to know one of the Sidhe, *you must remember never to tell a lie about them.*

Red Rory – or Rory Dearg as he was called because of his bright red hair – knew some of the sea-fairies. He was always good and kind to them and in return they helped him in many ways. But when he told a lie about them, they were very angry...

One evening in late September Rory Dearg and a few of his friends were sitting on the long pebbled beach tossing stones into the foaming waves. They were talking about the fairy folk, the *Sidhe*.

'They live in those caves over there,' Rory said, pointing out across the sea towards a small rocky island. Rory was a short, stout man, with a head of bright red hair and bushy eyebrows.

'How do you know?' Thomas, one of his neighbours, asked.

'Because I'm very friendly with the fairy folk,' Rory said proudly. He took a deep breath and smiled broadly. 'They often come over here and visit their relations that live in the fairy mounds.'

'And how do they get over here?' another neighbour asked.

Rory stood up and pointed down into the sea. 'There's a secret path, made of white sand and coral that runs along the sea bed from the island to the mainland,' he said.

'How do you know?' the neighbour asked.

Rory smiled again, his broad face breaking up into hundreds of tiny wrinkles. 'Because I've walked along that road with them.'

'You! What would the *Sidhe* folk want you for?'

'Why, to help carry their sacks of gold and silver across to their relations. They make it on the island, but because it's so heavy, they usually ask me to carry it for them.'

'And do they pay you?' Thomas asked.

'Of course they do,' Rory said.

'Well, let's see some fairy gold or silver then,' Thomas said.

Rory Dearg smiled secretively. 'Oh, it's neither gold nor silver that they pay me with.' He saw the looks of disbelief on their faces. 'Well, I'll tell you then – but you must swear never to tell, for they wouldn't like it if they knew I told anyone.' He waited until they had all promised, and then he whispered. 'They pay me with magic powers!'

'What sort of magic powers?' one of the men asked, curious now.

Rory looked across the waves towards the island. The sun was sinking down behind it and the water was shining red-gold. If you looked quickly at the island at this time of day, it was easy to imagine that it might be a fairy palace in disguise.

46

'What sort of magic powers?' the man asked again.

Rory looked at him. 'I really shouldn't say...'

'But we've promised,' the man said.

'Oh, all right then,' he said. 'They've given me *knowledge*.'

'*Knowledge*? What sort of knowledge?'

Rory Dearg shrugged. 'All sorts of knowledge. I can never be tricked now, because I'll be able to see through the trick. No one can ever lie to me, because I'll know it's a lie. Why, I even know the fairies' secrets!' He stuck his hands in his pockets and nodded importantly. 'Even they can't trick me!'

And that was a lie.

And what Rory Dearg didn't know was at that very moment, two of the tiny fairy folk were hiding in a small hollow in the ground under a broad flat stone just behind him.

The small group of friends and neighbours broke up as night fell and the first stars began to sparkle in the sky. Rory Dearg climbed up the little twisting path that led to his cottage. From the distance he could see the lights in the windows and he saw a shadow moving across them. That would be his wife Moire, preparing supper.

The track led down across two fields and then out onto a small track that led to his door, and Rory was just about to cross the first field when he felt a cold wind ruffle his hair. His skin prickled and his eyes stung with dust, making him squeeze them shut.

And when he opened his eyes again, the field was gone and in its place a broad, foaming river rushed past, heading down towards the sea.

Rory stopped in amazement, his eyes and mouth

open wide. What had happened? He looked around, but everything else seemed to be all right. He could still see the lights of his own cottage across the field – the river now, he corrected himself.

'How am I going to get home?' he asked aloud.

There was a sudden flapping of wings and Rory was shaken by a gust of wind. He looked up . . . just as a golden eagle folded its wings and dropped to the ground beside him. The bird was huge, far bigger than any eagle Rory had ever seen. Its plumage was a rich golden colour, shot through with bronze and copper feathers. Its claws were as thick as Rory's arm, and the bird was so heavy that they sank slightly into the earth. Its great black eyes blinked slowly as they stared at the frightened man. Suddenly it opened its beak and Rory jumped.

'I can help you,' it said, in a deep rich voice.

Rory could only stare in astonishment at the creature. He opened his mouth to say something, but nothing came out.

'I won't harm you.' The huge eagle took a step closer and raised his head until its eyes were almost on a level with Rory's.

The man tried to speak again, and he eventually said, 'You can speak!'

The eagle laughed, a deep, chuffing sound. 'Of course I can talk. All creatures can speak – but not all humans can hear them speak.'

Rory took a deep breath. 'What has happened to the field?' he said at last.

The golden eagle's wings shook. 'Fairy work that!' he said. 'You must have offended them somehow.'

'But I haven't done anything to them,' Rory protested.

The huge black eyes seemed to grow. 'But have

48

you said something about them, or spoken about them, or even told a lie about them?' The creature chuffed in laughter again. 'They don't like people telling lies about them.'

Rory Dearg suddenly remembered the stories he had told a little earlier. He felt his broad face burning with shame. He stuck his hands in his pockets and shuffled his feet. 'Well...' he began.

'Well?' the eagle said.

'Perhaps I did,' he said at last.

The giant eagle nodded. 'Perhaps you did.'

Rory looked across the river towards his home, and then he looked back at the eagle. 'Could you help me?' he asked.

'That's why I'm here,' the eagle said. 'Climb up onto my back and I'll carry you across.'

Rory looked at the huge eagle and hesitated. He had often heard stories about eagles – and golden eagles especially – carrying human children off to their nests. This eagle was so big he could easily carry a fully grown man. He looked at the fast-flowing river again. 'I might be able to swim,' he said doubtfully.

The eagle chuffed again. 'You would be swept away to the sea.'

Rory nodded. 'I suppose you're right.' He walked around behind the huge bird and, taking a fistful of gleaming feathers, he hoisted himself up onto its broad back and settled behind the wings.

'Are you ready now?' the eagle asked.

Rory felt his heart begin to pound hard against his chest. 'I'm ready,' he said in a high-pitched squeak.

The eagle spread his wings and the man felt the bird's body tense and then with two powerful flaps, the bird seemed to leap straight up into the air. Rory shouted and gripped the eagle's feathers all the more tightly as the earth just fell away beneath him. He squeezed his eyes shut.

Rory Dearg opened his eyes again when the huge bird stopped moving. He expected to see his own small white-washed cottage, with its two lighted windows and a curl of white smoke rising from the chimney – but what he did see was a barren, rocky mountainside, with nothing but grey stone covered with grey dust stretching in all directions. Above the mountain the sky was a purple-black colour and the stars were hard and sharp and brilliant.

With a heave of its shoulder muscles, the eagle threw him off. Rory landed with a thump in the soft grey dust. It rose up in a slow, swirling cloud and then gently fell around him, covering him in grey. He looked up at the eagle in astonishment. 'Where have you brought me – and why?'

The eagle laughed its chuffing laugh. 'The fairies asked me to do them a favour,' he said. 'You shouldn't have told that lie about them.' The bird turned its great head and looked at the desolate landscape. 'These are the Mountains of the Moon,' he said.

'But how am I going to get home?' Rory cried.

The eagle shrugged. 'I don't know.' It pointed with one of its massive wings. 'Don't go over there though,' it said, 'otherwise you might just fall off this world.' It paused and then added, with a chuff, 'It's flat, you see.' The golden bird chuffed again, and then rose up on its powerful wings, causing the grey dust to rise and billow – and when the dust had cleared, the bird was gone.

Rory sat on the ground and held his head. He felt like screaming and shouting and crying, but after a while, he got up and made his way across the dusty ground towards a series of low jagged hills, to the spot where the eagle had told him not to go.

He stopped when he reached them and looked down in amazement. There was nothing beyond the hills. The ground dropped down, down, down ... like a cliff. And he couldn't see the bottom.

He heard a noise behind him and spun around. There was no one there, but even as he watched, the dust began to shift and rise, and then a square door in the side of one of the low hills opened and a small, grey-skinned, grey-haired and grey-eyed man came out. He was wearing a long grey robe and carrying a tall stick of grey wood.

'Go away,' he said, in a dry cracked voice.

'But...' Rory began.

'I don't want to listen to any excuses,' the grey man said. 'Go away.'

'Where do I go?' Rory managed to say at last.

'I don't know,' the grey man said, 'but just go away.'

'Well, you'll have to help me,' Rory said firmly.

The grey man smiled a grey smile. 'I'll help you,' he said and took a step nearer Rory. 'Go away,' he suddenly said, and struck him in the chest with his stick.

Rory toppled backwards, his arms twirling, and then the edge of the cliff crumbled away and he sailed out off the edge of the Mountains of the Moon – and fell.

'And don't lie about the fairies again,' the grey man called after him.

Rory fell and fell and fell and fell, down, down, down and down. He saw the stars go flashing by, and then this huge blue-white ball came at him. He tried to duck – but suddenly he was inside the ball and still falling. It was hot and then cold, dry and then wet as he went through a fluffy-white cloud – and then he realised that he was falling back to earth!

Rory saw many shapes moving beneath him, forming one long V shape. He was just beginning to wonder what it was when he crashed into it. It was a flock of geese.

'Help!' he shouted.

'Why?' a bubbly voice asked.

'Because I'm falling,' he screamed.

'Then you shouldn't have jumped,' the same bubbly voice said, but something caught the neck of his shirt and he hung, arms and legs dangling and the ground far, far below.

Rory looked up into the long flat head of a wild goose. Its heavy black beak was holding onto the neck of his shirt. 'I didn't jump,' he said at last, and then he told the goose what had happened.

The kindly creature nodded, and said in its muffled, bubbly voice (because it couldn't open its beak), 'The fairies don't like to be lied about. This is their way of getting their own back.'

'Help me to get home please,' Rory said, 'and I promise that there will be a place for every goose and gander in the pond at the end of my field. And I'll never tell another lie about the *Sidhe*.'

The goose nodded. 'Well, I'll do the best I can, but you're a long way from home. I might not be able to carry you all the way back.'

However, the goose flew on, its wings beating slowly and powerfully on the cold air. They flew through clouds that were thin and cold, and others that were warm and dry. Sometimes they even flew above the clouds, so that, looking down, they seemed like fluffy balls of wool.

At last the goose said to Rory, 'I can't hold on to

you any longer. I'll have to let you go here, but you're above water and not too far from the land of Erin.'

'You can't let me go!' Rory shouted, but it was too late. He fell again, down, down, and down. He fell through a cloud and just had time to shout with surprise when he saw something blue and white come rushing up to meet him – and he splashed into the sea. He seemed to be going down for ages, when he struck something that was both warm and solid. The thump jarred every bone in his body, and he held on with all his might as the ground began to move up towards the surface.

When it broke through the waves, he found he was lying on the back of a huge whale. Its tiny black eyes looked back at him, and, Rory thought, if a whale were able to have an expression on its face, this one would have looked annoyed.

'Eating I was, having a snack,' the whale boomed suddenly, 'minding my own business, not even chasing the fishes, when what happens, you come crashing into me...'

I'm sorry,' Rory said, 'I didn't mean...'

'Oh, I know. I'll bet you didn't mean to tell lies about the fairies, but you did. Well, don't think we don't know about it.' The whale paused and seemed to take a deep breath. 'Now, get off my back!'

'I can't,' Rory said, 'I can't swim.'

'Of course you can,' the whale boomed, 'everyone can swim.'

'But I can't,' Rory said again, 'I never learnt!'

'Well, it's about time you did then,' the whale said – and spouted. A thin gush of water suddenly shot out of the blow-hole on the top of his head. It caught Rory in the seat of his trousers and pushed him up into the air. He closed his eyes feeling the rush of wind past his face...

And when he opened them again, he was lying on his back on the beach with his wife standing over him with an empty bucket in one hand and a towel in the other which she was shaking in his face.

Rory told his wife the story, and he told many of his friends and neighbours the same story over the next few days - but no one believed him. They all said that he must have fallen asleep on the beach and dreamt it all.

Rory himself might have agreed with them - except for two strange things: the grey dust in his pockets and the golden eagle's feather that was stuck in his coat!

CHAPTER SIX

The Fairy Dance

Time is different in fairy land: what may seem to be only hours there might be years in this world. This is a story about a young girl who goes into that magical land...

Paul sat up in bed suddenly. He could hear music coming from outside. He knew it was late because the house was very, very quiet, and the moonbeam, which had slanted in through his window when he went to bed, was now around over the other side of the room.

He got up out of bed and tiptoed over to the window and peered out. The full moon lit up everything in a ghostly silver-white light, and somehow made the shadows seem even darker.

But he could see no one.

He listened hard, trying to fix the direction of the sound. It was a thin, high sound, much like that of a pipe or flute, or perhaps even the delicate sound of a harp – and it seemed to be coming from the little clump of trees that lay at the bottom of the field.

Paul suddenly shivered, not with the cold but with excitement. He crept back to his bed and began pulling on his shirt and trousers, grabbing his cardigan as he slipped from the room.

In the next room, his sister Brona tossed and turned in her sleep. She was dreaming about a waterfall and the musical sound it made as it splashed into the pool beneath. And then she dreamt that she was standing on a plank of wood that was being tossed around on a stormy sea. Suddenly the wood tilted and she fell off – and woke up. Her brother Paul was shaking her.

'Wake up, wake up,' he whispered.

'What's wrong?' she mumbled, wondering what time it was.

'Music,' he said excitedly. 'I can hear music from outside.'

'What time is it?' she demanded, coming more awake, and realising how dark the room was.

'Oh, it's very late. Everyone's gone to bed, and the moon is beginning to sink.'

'It must be three in the morning,' Brona said angrily, pushing herself up into a sitting position. She was a year older than her brother, and liked to consider herself more grown up.

'That doesn't matter,' Paul said. 'Someone is playing music outside,' he said slowly and distinctly.

'At three o'clock in the morning?' Brona said in amazement. 'You're dreaming!'

'Listen,' he said. 'Just listen.'

Brona listened. And she too heard the music.

She hopped out of bed and together she and Paul stood on either side of the window peering out from behind the curtains. 'I think it's coming from over there,' Paul said, pointing down towards the trees.

His sister nodded. 'I think so too.'

'Let's go and look,' Paul said.

'But the time...' his sister began.

'Tomorrow's Saturday – we don't have to be up for school, and no one will know. We'll just creep out by the back door and have a look. It might be a gypsy caravan,' he added excitedly.

'Or the Fairy Host,' Brona whispered.

'Fairy Host!' Paul laughed quietly. He didn't believe in fairies. He wasn't too sure about ghosts, though.

Brother and sister crept down the garden path, keeping in close to the bushes and making for the wooden gate. The music was louder now, and once they thought they heard the distant sounds of voices and laughter.

They slipped through the gate and headed down the path towards the sounds of the music. It was louder and clearer now, and the voices were much clearer also. Paul and Brona stopped and listened. The language was not English and although it sounded something like Irish, they weren't able to make out what was being said.

'I think it's gypsies,' Paul said, 'and that must be their secret language, *Shelta*.'

Brona shook her head. 'I don't think so,' she whispered. 'It sounds... almost familiar.' She looked over at her brother, her eyes shining silver in the moonlight. 'It's almost as if we should know it,' she said.

Paul nodded. There was something about the language...

They crept through the bushes and down along the banks of a tiny stream that ran past the foot of their garden. There were three broad, flat stones that they used as stepping stones, and once over these they were into the fringes of the little forest.

Long thin beams of moonlight slanted in through the branches of the trees, speckling the ground with patches of deep shadow, making it almost impossible for them to see where they were going.

Suddenly Brona laid her hand on Paul's arm. He jumped and bit his lip in fright.

'What's that?' she whispered, and he could just make out the shape of her arm pointing straight ahead.

Paul squinted in the direction she was pointing. For a moment he could see nothing, and then he saw a light – more of a dim glow really – between the trees. A cloud slid across the face of the moon, and the little forest went absolutely black, and they suddenly found that they could see the glow all the more clearly, and, at the same time, the sound of the music and laughter seemed to increase.

Holding each other's hands they crept towards the glow.

There was a sudden blare of trumpets, and everything lit up like a firework, with streamers of coloured light darting and slipping through the trees and into the heavens. There were red and green and blue sparks cartwheeling and spinning along the forest floor, and ribbons of what looked like fire – although they didn't seem to burn – snaked along the little pathways.

The young boy and girl were suddenly very frightened. Paul tugged on his sister's hand. 'Come on – let's go,' he hissed.

She shook her head and pulled her hand free. 'No – listen!'

'I can't hear anything…' he began, but she squeezed his hand tight, and he shut up. He listened again, and then he heard it, faint and distant but becoming clearer – the brittle sound of horses' hooves. They crouched down into the bushes and huddled together.

There was a flash of movement down along the path and then the bushes parted and two creatures marched into the little clearing. They were small, stout men, dressed in bright red waistcoats, with long heavy green coats over them. They wore old fashioned three-cornered hats, green tights, and beautifully made shoes with huge silver buckles on their feet.

'*Leprechauns!*' Brona whispered in astonishment.

The two leprechauns held back the bushes as a dozen tiny winged creatures hurried past them and then fluttered up into the low branches of the trees that lined the path.

And then the horses and their riders came into the clearing.

There were two of them. Both horses were tall and thin, with sharp angular features and long pointed ears. Their eyes were huge and glowed brightly, and were slit-pupilled, like a cat's.

Their riders were equally strange. The man was very tall, with a sharp, pointed face and snow-white hair. His clothes were old-fashioned, but beautifully made and of the best fabrics, and there was a sword with a blade of what looked like glass tied to his high saddle.

He was followed by a woman; a small, delicate woman who looked no older than Brona – except for her eyes, which were very old indeed. Her cheekbones were high and her eyes almost slanted. Her hair was silver-white and flowed down her back in a long shimmering wave. Like the man, she was dressed in the fashion of another age, in a long, trailing gown of green silk, that was decorated

along the hem and about the neck and sleeves with an ancient Celtic design.

'Who... who are they?' Paul whispered into his sister's ear.

'They are the Shining Folk, the *Sidhe*, the Tuatha De Danann,' Brona murmured, almost as much to herself as to her brother.

'Fairies?'

Brona nodded. 'Fairies. That must be their king and queen.'

'But what are they doing here?' Paul asked.

His sister shrugged. 'I don't know. It must be one of their gatherings, when all the fairy folk came together to sing and dance through the night. You know,' Brona insisted, 'you often see the rings of pale grass in the mornings, or circles of mushrooms that have sprung up overnight.'

Paul nodded. 'I've seen them.'

The lord and lady of the *Sidhe* rode slowly past the bushes which hid the boy and girl, although Brona thought she saw the lady glance down as she passed and smile at their hiding place. The two leprechauns hurried past and once again held back the bushes to allow them to ride into the wide glowing circle.

Paul and Brona caught a glimpse of the gathering before the leprechauns stepped through and allowed the bushes to drop back. In that instant they had seen a huge gathering of creatures and beings from Ireland's mythology: there were not only leprechauns, but cluricauns, fir dearg, fir bolg, tall, wild-haired women with sorrowful eyes, that they guessed must be the dreaded banshee. There were animals also, huge dogs, long-horned cows, bright-eyed hares and rabbits and a wild-maned, savage-looking horse, that they knew must be the terrible Phooka, the demon-horse.

When the bushes closed on the scene, the music began once again – a thin, high, very delicate sound. Other musical instruments joined in and soon the tiny forest was alive with sound.

Paul tugged on his sister's arm. 'Come on, let's go.'

'Not yet. Let's get closer.'

Paul shook his head. 'Don't be silly. We're lucky they didn't spot us when they rode past. What do you think would happen if they caught us?'

Someone began to sing in the clearing, and the shouting and laughter died down as the haunting voice drifted out over the land. It was so beautiful that Brona shivered with the sound of it.

'Brona... please,' Paul asked, 'can we go?'

'I wonder who's singing,' his sister said softly. 'I'll bet it's the fairy queen...' she got up on her hands and knees and began to creep towards the clearing.

'Brona, don't!' Paul hissed, but she just ignored him and continued crawling towards the light and sound.

She was nearly there when the song finished and the Fairy Host cried aloud in its strange language, applauding the singer. Then someone began to beat a drum, and an instrument that sounded like bagpipes started up, and then trumpets joined in and soon the whole company was singing and swirling around to the dance music.

Paul felt his heart begin to pound in time to the music and he pressed his hands to his ears to try and shut out the sounds. But he could still feel the music throbbing up through the ground.

It made him want to dance...

63

Brona! He looked for his sister. He could just about make out her shape outlined against the bushes ahead of him. She was swaying in time to the music and even as he looked she began to part the bushes that hid her from the Fairy Host...

'No!' he shouted, but he couldn't be heard above the throbbing of the music. He scrambled forward, but he was too late. Brona had joined in the fairy dance.

And then the whole clearing lit up with a ghostly coloured fire, and he fell back covering his stinging eyes. When he could see again, the Fairy Host, and his sister were gone.

There was a big search for Brona, but she was never found. No one believed Paul's story. He had been dreaming, they said, and eventually his family moved away from the village and settled in Dublin where the fairy folk were spoken of only with a smile. Paul grew up and moved away from Ireland, travelling all over the world, but always promising to return to the village of his childhood.

The old white-haired man made his way down the track that led to the stream. In sixty years it hadn't changed much – except that it seemed much smaller now than it had once seemed to a nine-year-old boy. He stopped and looked back; the house was still there, of course. It was boarded up now, with slates missing from the roof and paint peeling off the walls. But it was more or less as he remembered it. He turned his back on it and continued on down towards the stream.

The old man paused by the edge of the little stream. Had it really shrunk, or had it just seemed much wider when he was a boy? The stepping stones were still there, and he crossed quickly to the far side. The forest hadn't changed at all. It still looked as dark and forbidding as it always had.

He shrugged and followed the winding animal track that led through the trees. The afternoon was very quiet and warm and he loosened his collar. He was glad he hadn't brought an umbrella. Once he stepped away from the stream the sound of water disappeared and he could only hear the distant trilling of a thrush.

And then it stopped and the afternoon was silent.

He heard the strange sound then. He stopped and listened, tilting his head from side to side and squinting into the bushes. He had just about decided that it was probably the sound of the water behind him when he heard it again - it was the sound of a child crying.

The old man pushed his way through the bushes and came out into a clearing - and found himself facing a young girl. She had her head buried in her hands and was crying bitterly - but he would have recognised the bright red hair anywhere.

'Brona?' he whispered.

The girl jumped with fright. When she looked up, her face was blotchy from crying and her eyes were red and swollen. 'Who are you?' she sniffed.

'Brona!' he said, 'it's you!'

'Yes, I'm Brona. Who are you?' the young girl asked. She looked hard at the old man. 'You look familiar, but I don't think I've ever seen you before.'

'We met a long time ago,' the old man whispered.

'When?' Brona demanded. 'I don't think I've met you.' She stood up and brushed grass and straw off her dress. 'And now I really must be getting home, my mother and father will be getting worried . . .'

The old man shook his head. 'They're not looking

for you,' he said softly. She opened her mouth to ask a question, but he held up his hand. 'What do you last remember?' he asked softly.

'I remember the Fairy Host, and dancing, dancing, dancing with them. My brother wouldn't dance with them though, but I danced the whole night through with them.'

'Brona,' the old man said gently, 'I am your brother Paul, you've been away with the fairies for more than sixty years!'

Brona lived with her brother Paul for many years afterwards. They moved away to Dublin where everyone thought that they were uncle and niece. Brona later became a famous dancer for she danced, and even walked, with beautiful grace and poise.

There is a country saying that anyone who has danced with the fairies, will hear their music forever after.

CHAPTER SEVEN

The Wise Woman's Payment

It is not wise to make an enemy of one of the Little Folk, because they can be very cruel and spiteful when they are annoyed. However, a leprechaun can be a very good friend to have. They are usually kind and considerate, and are always full of good advice.

Nano Hayes was a wise woman, a mna allthacha. She knew all the herbs that could cure, and she was even able to see into the future. If she made a cure from her huge stock of herbs, she only charged a few pence, and if the people hadn't got the money with them, she would tell them to drop it in when they were passing her cottage. Sometimes they forgot, and she was too kind-hearted to ask for it directly. And then there were other people, who just didn't bother paying at any time.

But she did manage to get payment of a sort in the end . . .

The old woman sat down on the hard, wooden chair and rested her elbows on the scratched wooden table. She looked at the small jar that sat on the table in front of her. 'That's all I have left,' she said, looking across towards the fireplace.

The small, dark man sitting there put down the

shoe he was mending and stuck his needle in the collar of his coat. He was called Seamus Ban and he was a leprechaun, a fairy shoemaker. 'What's all you have left?' he asked.

Nano Hayes picked up the small jar and shook it. Something rustled dryly inside. 'This is the last jar of healing herbs I have left,' she said.

'Where did the rest go to?' Seamus asked, his lined face crinkling up into a frown.

'Well, I've used them all,' Nano Hayes said. She was a small, frail woman, with a round, wrinkled face, and thick grey hair that matched the colour of her eyes. 'I used a lot last month when nearly everyone in the village caught that bad cold, and then there was that rash that the boys in the school got when they fell into those nettles...'

'How did you cure that?' Seamus asked. Leprechauns, because they were so small, were often stung by nettles.

'Well, I rubbed a fresh dock leaf on the sting,' Nano Hayes said, 'they're very good. But you can also bathe the sting with vinegar, especially apple-cider vinegar – and that's also very good for those blisters you get from poison ivy.'

'Now isn't that a strange thing,' Seamus Ban said, 'the Little Folk can handle poison ivy with no bad effects – although I know humans never should.'

'We must have different types of skin,' Nano Hayes said. She got up and went to the big cupboard on the wall. She picked up another jar and shook it. 'I've no walnuts either,' she said.

'What do you want walnuts for?' the leprechaun asked.

'The girls in the village often come to me looking for something to clear their skins and make their eyes bright and sparkling. Walnuts are very good for a clear skin.' She continued searching through the cupboard, shaking jars and putting them to one side. 'You boil about fifteen or twenty large walnuts in water, until the water starts to look dirty, and then you wash your face in the water.'

Seamus smiled. 'And what happens when you wash your face in this dirty water?' he asked rubbing his own dirty face.

Nano Hayes laughed. 'It's not dirty water. It's only the oils from the walnuts. It will clear up your skin in days. But if you don't like that, you can always use half an apple, a cucumber or a potato and rub them in against your skin.'

'The Little People always wash their faces in the first dew of a May morning, just before the sun rises,' the leprechaun said.

Nano Hayes nodded. 'Yes, humans can do that also.' She stepped back and closed the doors of her cupboard gently. In her hand she held another small jar.

'What's in that?' Seamus asked.

'Mint,' she said.

'We make a sort of tea out of mint,' he said.

'So do we,' the woman said. She crossed the room to the table and sat down again.

Seamus got up from his chair by the fire and sat down opposite her. 'Where have all the herbs gone?' he asked. 'Why haven't you bought more?'

'I've used them all,' she said, 'and no one has paid me for them yet. I can't buy any more because I've no money.' She shook her head. 'Anyway, I usually pick my own herbs fresh from the mountain and river sides; I only buy those you cannot find around here.'

Seamus looked thoughtful. 'So, why can't you go

out and pick them yourself?' he asked.

Nano Hayes shrugged again. 'Because I need so many – and because winter will soon be here and a lot of my herbs will be dead by then. I really must have them picked by the day after tomorrow at the latest.'

'Will the villagers not help you?' Seamus asked.

The old woman shook her head. 'I don't want to ask them.'

'But they ask you when they need help.'

'That's different,' Nano Hayes said.

'No, it's not.'

'Well, I'm not going to ask them to spend all day picking herbs, grasses, leaves and berries just for me,' she protested.

'Tell them it's your payment for all the cures they haven't paid for,' the leprechaun said.

'I couldn't do that,' she said in amazement.

'Well pay them then,' the small man said, smiling hugely.

'With what?' Nano Hayes asked, 'I've no money to buy herbs, so how can I offer to pay them?'

Seamus Ban smiled again, his wide grin almost splitting his face in two. He slipped off the chair and went back over to the fire, where he rummaged about in his brown cloth bag, which he carried everywhere.

'What are you doing?' the old wise woman asked.

'Looking.'

'Looking for what?'

'For this!' The leprechaun stood up with a heavy-looking brown bundle in his hand. He shook it and it gave a muffled clink.

Nano Hayes suddenly looked doubtful. 'If that's what I think it is...' she began.

Seamus climbed back up into the chair and placed the heavy bundle down on the wooden table. 'And what do you think it is?' he asked.

'I think it's leprechaun gold,' she said.

Seamus Ban laughed in his jolly voice. 'So that's why they call you a wise woman,' he said, opening the knot that held the bundle together, and pulling the cloth apart. A rich, warm golden-yellow glow lit up the dark room, for on the table were a hundred large golden coins.

Nano Hayes' mouth opened into a big 'O' of surprise. She had never seen so much money before in all her years. She touched it carefully with a finger, not sure whether it was real or not. But it chinked together like real money.

'You can have it,' Seamus Ban said.

The old woman looked shocked. 'I will not!'

But the leprechaun nodded insistently. 'Yes, you will. You've been good to the Little Folk, Nano, and you've never accepted anything for your help. Well, now we can help you – and you cannot refuse our help.'

'But it's such a lot of money,' the old woman said.

'But it's fairy gold,' Seamus Ban said, and winked.

And then the old woman understood and she smiled broadly. She picked up the four ends of the cloth and tied the money up in a neat bundle, and slipped it into her apron pocket.

That same afternoon, Nano Hayes walked into the village and told everyone she met that if they were to come up to her house at dawn the following morning, they would have a chance of making some money. Soon the whole village knew, and everyone was very curious to know how they were going to earn this money. But Nano Hayes would say nothing, only tell them to be outside her door at dawn.

The next morning there was a huge crowd outside Nano Hayes' cottage. The sky to the east was bright with the coming dawn, although overhead the stars still sparkled, and sunrise was still a little way away. Nearly everyone from the village was there, and the morning air was filled with a low buzz as they talked quietly amongst themselves, wondering why the old wise woman had brought them out so early.

A cock crowed on the cottage's thatched roof and the door opened. Nano Hayes walked out into the cold morning air. She was carrying a heavy-looking bundle that chinked and clinked as she walked.

'I would like to thank you all for coming here,' she said. 'I am pleased to see I have so many friends in the village.' She paused and looked at the faces. Most of them were looking at the bundle she held in her hand, wondering what it held.

'In the past few months,' she continued, 'I have used up all my healing herbs, and now, with winter fast approaching, I find I am very short. So I have asked you here today to help me pick the herbs, leaves, bark, berries, roots and weeds that I will need to make my cures.'

The crowd looked puzzled and some murmured angrily. This was not what they had expected.

'Of course,' Nano Hayes continued, 'I don't expect you to do this for nothing, and everyone who helps me will receive one gold piece.' She dipped her hand into the bundle and pulled out one shining gold coin and held it up.

The crowd murmured like a swarm of bees.

'Are there any questions?' she asked, putting the coin back into the bundle, where everyone heard it chink against the others.

'Yes,' someone in the crowd said. 'Where did you get all that money?'

Nano Hayes smiled widely. 'It's fairy gold,' she said.

So, for the rest of the day, the people of the village wandered up the hills and through the little valleys, looking for the herbs and roots for Nano Hayes. They looked for the bark of certain trees, and the berries from different bushes, they picked dandelions and mushrooms, and some even wandered down onto the beach to pick up seaweed for her.

Soon, a huge bundle of bits and pieces began to gather outside the wise woman's door, where she sat on a low, three-legged stool sorting everything out. By early afternoon, she had everything she needed for another year, but still it continued coming and by evening, when the sun was beginning to sink into the west, she had enough to last her for the next two years.

As the villagers began to trickle in, hot and tired, some scratched and bruised, Nano Hayes gave each of them a single gold coin, saying, 'Now, remember, this is fairy gold,' and then she would add, 'Do you owe anyone any money?'

Now a few people thought about it, and then they smiled shyly and handed the money back to the old woman, saying, 'That's for the medicine you made me a while ago.' But to these Nano Hayes would shake her head and press the coin back into their hand, and tell them that they had worked hard enough for their money.

But others would just look her straight in the eye and shake their heads and say that they owed no one any money.

By the time the first stars began to twinkle in the night sky, the last of the villagers had gone to their homes and the bag of money was empty. Nano Hayes and Seamus Ban stood by the door of her cottage and looked down at the lights of the village.

'Well now, wasn't that a good idea of mine?' the leprechaun asked, looking at the tied up bundles of herbs and grasses.

The old woman nodded. 'It certainly was. But it cost you a lot of money,' she said.

The small man shook his head and laughed. 'Not as much as you might think,' he said. 'Don't forget, that was fairy money you gave them.'

And then he and Nano Hayes went back inside, laughing.

Fairy money is a strange thing. The next morning, those people who had lied and said that they owed nothing, found that their fairy money had turned to a lump of stone.

CHAPTER EIGHT

The Fairy Harper

In the old times, the fairies would sometimes creep into a house where there was a new-born boy and exchange it for one of their own. These children were called changelings, and were often ugly and mischievous. But they usually had a gift - and if you could find that gift, you would be able to use it to send them back to fairy land and bring back the human child...

Grania O'Neill stood by the side of the wooden cradle and looked down into it. Her neighbour and friend, Sheila, looked over her shoulder.

'What are you going to call him?' Sheila asked.

Grania tucked the blue blanket in around the tiny baby's chin, and slipped his arms beneath the covers. 'We'll call him Brian, I think,' she said.

Sheila nodded. 'His grandfather is called Brian, isn't he?' She peeped into the cot again. 'Who do you think he looks like?'

Grania shook her head. 'I don't know.' She frowned slightly. 'When he was born I thought he looked like me, and I could have sworn he had reddish hair then.' She ran her fingers through the child's mop of dark hair. 'I must have been mistaken though.'

Sheila glanced down into the cot again and frowned. 'His hair is black,' she said. 'Are you sure it was red when he was born – it wasn't just the light?'

Grania shook her head. 'No, I remember thinking that his hair was the same colour as mine...' she paused. 'You don't think anything's wrong?' she asked.

Her neighbour quickly shook her head. 'No... no, of course not.'

The tiny baby whimpered in his sleep and turned over.

As the years passed, it became very clear that young Brian O'Neill was different from his two brothers and father. They were big and broad and all three had heads of bright red hair. Brian was thin and spindly and his hair was black.

By the time he was five years old, he was a difficult boy, always trying to cause trouble between his brothers, breaking things, telling lies, throwing stones at the dogs and cats. Grania tried to control her son, but it wasn't easy, and her husband, Mark, was out most of the day, tending to the farm with his two older sons.

Now one day, just before Brian's sixth birthday, an old blind harper came to the village. He was called Turlough Carolan – and he was the finest harper in all Ireland, if not the world.

News of the harper's arrival travelled quickly through the village. Carolan was a very famous man, and welcomed everywhere he went, for wherever he went there was sure to be a party.

Sheila came running up to the O'Neill household, 'The harper's come,' she shouted, 'and there's to be a dance tonight in the field beyond the village.'

'Which harper?' Grania asked, 'surely not Turlough Carolan?'

Sheila nodded. 'Yes, Carolan the Harper. Now will you come tonight?' she asked. 'I'll be there.'

Grania nodded. 'I would love to...' and then she paused, 'but what about Brian?'

'Bring him with you,' Sheila said, 'it's probably the only time the harper will come through our village.'

Grania nodded. 'We'll be there,' she said.

So, shortly after tea that day, Grania dressed Brian in clean clothes, while her husband and two older sons also dressed themselves in their best clothes, and then the family headed off into the village towards the field.

By the time they reached the village it was deserted, but in the distance they could hear a low murmuring and, every now and again, the faint sound of a harp.

When they reached the field they found that everyone from the village and nearby houses and cottages had come to hear the legendary harper. Some of the shop-keepers had set up wooden tables and there were baskets of fruit and freshly baked bread for sale, and some people even had huge pots of tea brewing. It was like a giant picnic.

Grania took Brian by the hand and made her way through the crowd to the far end of the field to where an ancient oak tree stood. The tree had once been struck by lightning and had burnt away to a tall twisted stump that looked like a hand closed into a fist, but with the first and little fingers pointing up towards the sky. Between these two pieces of wood there was a sort of natural seat, and the harper was sitting there.

There was quite a crowd around Turlough

Carolan. He was a small, stout man, bald and with a pleasant round face that was fringed with tufts of white hair. He was dressed in clothes that had once been fine, but which were now well-worn. There were patches on the elbows and knees and Grania noticed that the sole of one of his shoes had come off, but he was cheerful and seemed to be laughing all the time. His poor clothes didn't seem to bother him.

His hands, Grania noticed, were lovely. They were long and slender, and his little finger was almost as long as his first. His nails were short, but spotlessly clean, and there were hard pads of skin on the tips of all his fingers from the strings of his harp. His harp was also very beautiful. He carried it in a plain soft leather bag, with a simple design running down one side and held closed by two strings. The body of the harp was made of plain black wood, inlaid with a Celtic design in gold, and there were tiny figures of men and animals carved down one side.

When the harper lifted up his harp, the crowd fell silent, and crowded around the small man. He looked up, his blind eyes seeming to look at each one in turn.

'Now, if you'll be so kind as to give me a little room here,' he said, in a soft, rich voice.

The crowd shuffled back and Carolan waited until they had moved far enough away. He then took his harp and settled it between his legs and then gently touched the strings. The sound it made was almost silent, and yet it hung on the air like the whistle of a breeze. The crowd sighed – all except Brian.

When he heard the first sounds from the harp, he stiffened and his dark eyes opened wide in astonishment. He squeezed his mother's hand so tightly that she let it go, and then he stood, swaying slightly in time to the music with both hands pressed to his cheeks.

Turlough Carolan played his harp. He played jigs and reels, happy songs, sad songs, old songs and some he had composed himself. He played quickly and then slowly, softly, then loudly. And all the time Brian O'Neill swayed in time to the music. When the harper played fast, the little boy would bounce around and jump up and down; and when the harper played a slow, sad song, the boy even cried.

Some time later the harper took a break. Someone brought him a drink, and he put down his harp and sat back against the ancient tree to rest. The people drifted off into small crowds, laughing and talking together, and no one noticed the small boy creeping towards the harp. He looked up, but Carolan was busy answering questions, with his harp leaning against the tree-stump. Brian reached out and touched the strings with his long, delicate fingers . . .

The first sounds were like a bugle call. Everyone in the field fell silent and turned towards the sound. Then a series of sharp, clear notes rang out, followed by a quick piece of difficult dance music. Some people began to clap, thinking it was the harper again but Carolan was just as surprised as everyone else.

Grania O'Neill turned when she heard the sounds. She got a fright when she saw her son handling the harp. She was about to reach out and pull him away when the harper's surprisingly strong fingers closed around her sleeve. She turned and looked into his blind eyes.

'Leave the boy,' he whispered, 'let him play.'

Grania looked from him to Brian and then back to

the harper. 'How do you know it's a boy?' she asked in amazement.

Carolan smiled. 'A boy plays differently to a girl; he has a different type of touch. When you cannot see, you make your other senses work all the harder. Even though people were talking to me, I heard someone approach my harp. I guessed then that it was a boy, and when I heard him play, I knew.' Carolan smiled quickly again. 'I heard you take a deep breath when you saw who was playing and then I heard you hurrying towards him.' He shrugged his shoulders. 'It's really quite easy.'

Grania shivered. 'It's almost like magic.'

Carolan shook his head. 'No, that's magic,' he said nodding towards the small boy playing the harp. 'Has he been playing long?' he asked.

Grania shook her head, and then, realising that the harper couldn't see, she said, 'No, no, this is the first time he has ever touched a harp.'

Turlough Carolan started. He squeezed Grania's arm tightly. 'The first time? He's never touched a harp before?'

'Never,' Grania said.

The harper looked troubled. 'Is there ... is everything right with the child? Does he look like the rest of your family?' he asked at last.

'No,' Grania whispered, and then she told Carolan about her son. When she was finished the harper remained silent for a while, but then he smiled sadly, and said, 'Well, we will have to see what we can do now, won't we?'

'I don't know what you mean,' Grania said.

'Don't you worry about it,' Carolan said. 'Let's just listen to the boy play for a while.'

And while Grania and Carolan had been talking, Brian had been playing the harp. His fingers danced across the strings, touching, stroking, brushing, pulling, plucking each one perfectly, as if he had been playing the harp all his life. He played tune after tune, some fast, some slow, some that people knew, and others that were wild and strange.

And when he played these tunes everyone felt their feet begin to tingle and then begin to tap, and they felt as if they had to dance. When Brian saw this, he began to play more and more of this wild, breezy music, and soon everyone was whirling about the field, dancing, dancing, dancing – even if they didn't want to!

Brian laughed then. 'Dance, dance, dance,' he called. He played fast and everyone fairly flew about the field in a dizzy circle, and then he played slow music, and everyone was forced to shuffle. But nobody could stop.

Then Carolan stretched out his hand, and said something in the old Irish language. Immediately the music stopped – and so did all the dancers, frozen into position. Brian touched the strings again and again, but no sound came from them. He looked over at the old harper. 'What have you done?' he demanded.

Carolan smiled. 'My harp obeys me – and only me.'

Brian plucked the strings again, but they hung slack like pieces of wool. 'Make it play!' he shouted.

Then the harper held out both hands and said something in the old language again. The harp seemed to tremble in Brian's hands, and then it began to shake, and suddenly it flew from his grip like a bird and landed safely in the harper's hands. Carolan stroked the strings, whispering gently to it, like a pet.

'Give it to me,' Brian shouted. He stood up and ran

towards the old man. But Carolan just smiled and touched the strings, sending out a thin, shivery sound that stopped the boy suddenly. He tilted his head up and looked from side to side, as if he was listening.

And then Carolan played. His music now was sad and strange, almost lost. The dancers – who were still frozen, though they were able to see and hear – felt the hairs on the backs of their necks begin to itch. They felt a cold wind that smelt faintly of roses and mint touch their skins and most of them suddenly felt very frightened.

They all knew that there was magic in the air.

The harper's music grew wilder. Clouds began to scuttle across the sky, hiding the moon and the stars which were beginning to shine, and it seemed to grow very dark, very quickly.

Suddenly there was the sound of many hooves, as if a troop of horses was approaching. The music quickened and it began to sound like people speaking.

A shape moved through the frozen people, looking like a tall, thin man on horseback. It moved between the harper and Brian, and then, suddenly, it was gone in a clatter of hooves – and so was the boy.

But in his place was a young human girl – with a head of bright red hair...

Afterwards people said that the harper's music was so beautiful that the fairy folk had been forced to come to its call. But some said that Carolan had learned to play from the Sidhe, *and that he was very friendly with them, and that they brought the girl back because he had asked them.*

Grania and Mark O'Neill called the young girl Nora. She was the baby that had been changed shortly after she had been born. She grew up to be a wise woman, a mna allthacha, *and she could do all sorts of cures. But she never liked the sound of a harp - isn't that strange?*

CHAPTER NINE

The Floating Island

There are supposed to be islands off the west coast of Ireland which float. These are fairy, magical islands, which rise up out of the sea once in every seven years...

Louisa loved to walk on the beach late in the evening when the sun was sinking down beneath the waves. She loved the colours of the sunset, the reds of the sea, the pinks of the sky and the blues, greens and purples of the clouds. And every sunset was different. The young girl would sit on the stony beach, with her chin resting on her knees and her arms wrapped around her legs, and watch the sun sink slowly into the wild western ocean.

Autumn was the best time for sunsets. In summer the sun rarely went down until far too late in the evening, and the sunsets then were not really brilliant, and in winter the weather was often bad and sometimes she didn't see the sun all day. But autumn was a really special time.

Louisa was nine years old, and she lived on Ireland's wild western coast, quite close to the huge, black Cliffs of Moher with her mother, father, older brothers and grandfather. She could look out of her bedroom window onto the Atlantic Ocean, and she would sometimes lie in bed and watch the birds flying past her window, coming in from the sea, and she often wondered whether they had flown all the way from America without a stop.

One evening in late September, she was walking on the beach waiting for the sun to set. It was already low over the sea. The sky had changed from a deep blue to a light, hazy purple colour, and some of the clouds were tinged with pink. Louisa climbed up onto a large, flat stone and settled back against it. The stone was still warm from the day's heat, and she closed her eyes and rested her head against the smooth rock. She was a tall, thin girl, with long, thick, black hair that fell to her back. Her face was round and her nose slightly turned up. Her eyes were the colour of grass.

She opened her eyes and looked up into the darkening sky. Far, far above her head, a long V-shape of birds flew slowly across the sky, little more than black dots in the distance. She turned back towards the sinking sun... and then she sat up suddenly. There was something out in the sea.

Louisa stood up on the flat stone and shaded her green eyes. 'What is it?' she wondered aloud.

She could see a long low shape in the water, not big enough to be a ship and too long to be a fishing boat, and Louisa didn't think it was a whale. She stopped and shook her head, squeezing her eyes shut and then looking again. The shape was coming closer.

'What is it?' she asked again. She climbed down off the rock, and hurried down the beach, the round stones rattling and clinking under her bare feet. Soon she was standing in the shallow water, her face screwed up tight and her hands shading her eyes from the glare of the sun. The shape was closer now ...

'It's an island!' she said in astonishment. But there was no island off the coast here. The next stretch of land after the Cliffs of Moher was the east coast of America, over a thousand miles away. Even as she watched little lights began to glow on the island, and then she found that they helped her to make out the shape. There was an old-fashioned type of house on the island – and, yes, she was right, the island was floating!

And it was coming closer.

Suddenly the sun disappeared beneath the horizon. She had been so intent on watching the strange shape that she had missed the sunset, but now, with the sun no longer blinding her eyes, she found she could see the island and the building quite clearly. The building was a long, low square shape with a low, sloping roof. It seemed to be made out of flat stones set one on top of the other, with huge stones at the bottom and smaller stones set on top. Louisa remembered her father building a wall the same way only a few weeks ago, and he had told her then that it was one of the oldest and safest ways of building a strong wall. He had also told her that some of the most ancient buildings had been made that way.

The stones of the building were wet and dripping and there were strands of seaweed hanging from the higher stones. There was a low wall, which had been made the same way, running around one part of the floating island, and a few small bushes and a couple of ragged, spindly trees, which were also dripping seaweed. The island had a rough stony beach, and Louisa could see a few silver fish flapping on the stones, where they must have been trapped when the island had risen from the sea.

Louisa knew then that it was a fairy island. She had often heard her grandfather tell about the islands of Tir na nOg and Hy-Brasil which were supposed to lie off the west coast of Ireland, and drift about in a fog bank. She remembered the old man telling her about the other islands which were part of the *Tir faoi Thuinn*, the Land Beneath the Waves, which sometimes rose up from the bottom of the sea and drifted about for a little while before sinking back to the sea-bed again. This must be one of those, she decided.

She wondered if any of the fairy folk actually lived on the island. She knew that there were people in the sea, Mer-Folk and Seal-Folk, and Sea-Horses and Sea-Cows, but did people actually live on the island beneath the waves? She looked closely at the island again.

'I wonder who lit the lamps?' she asked aloud.

'*I did.*'

Louisa jumped. She turned around quickly, but there was no one there – she was the only one on the beach. She turned back to the island.

'Who are you?' she asked, and then she said, 'Where are you?'

The door in the building on the island opened, throwing a long beam of yellow light out across the water. A tall, thin figure stepped into the light and raised its arm in a wave.

'I am the Woman of the Isle,' the figure said, and then Louisa realised that the woman had not actually spoken aloud. The girl had heard her inside her head. 'I will not harm you,' the woman said.

Louisa hugged herself tightly. It suddenly seemed to have turned very cold. 'What is your name?' she asked.

The Woman of the Isle stepped out of the light and walked slowly down the thin white path that led to the beach. Louisa saw that she was very pale indeed, although both her skin and hair had a slightly greenish colour. She was wearing a gown that looked like it was made up out of long strands of different-coloured seaweed, and she had a simple coral crown on her head. She stopped on the beach, close to the edge of the water, and the island had now drifted so close that there was very little distance between the girl on the shore and the woman on the island.

'I have no name,' she said at last, and although she didn't move her lips, Louisa heard her quite clearly. She saw her frown. 'No, that is not true; I had a name once, but it was a long, long time ago, and it has been so long since I used it that I must admit that I've forgotten what my name was. What is yours?' she asked.

Louisa hesitated. Names were supposed to have a little magic in them, and if she told this strange woman her name, would she then have power over her?

'I will not harm you,' the Woman of the Isle said slowly inside Louisa's head.

The girl nodded to herself. 'My name is Louisa,' she said.

The Woman on the Isle frowned. 'Louisa... Louisa... Louisa,' she repeated slowly. 'What a strange, beautiful name,' she said. 'I have never heard it before.'

'Surely you can remember your own name?' Louisa asked quietly.

The woman shook her head. 'It has been so long... so long.' She pressed her pale hands to her head and thought hard. At last she looked up. 'It

might have been Rhian,' she said.

'Rhian,' Louisa said, pronouncing the strange word slowly. 'Rhian. It is a very lovely name.'

The woman smiled. 'It is a very ancient name.'

'Are you very old too?' the girl asked.

Rhian smiled a little. 'Very old,' she said.

The island bumped against the shore with a crunch of sand and stones, and then stopped. Rhian reached out her hand. 'Would you like to see my island?' she asked.

Louisa hesitated for a few moments. It was getting late and she knew she should be home... but then she decided that if she only went over for a few moments, no one would know. Louisa reached out her hand and hopped up onto the rocky beach of the island.

Rhian, the Woman of the Isle, showed her over the small island. She showed her the bare trees that only flowered once in every hundred years and only bore fruit once in every thousand years – but if you managed to eat some of that fruit you would become immortal – you would live forever. She showed her bushes whose leaves could be woven into the finest cloth, and there was a sort of grass on the island that could be cut and shaped into warm, fleecy blankets.

And then she showed the girl her house.

From the outside it looked like nothing more than a rough stone building with a thick wooden door, but from the inside it was far, far different. Louisa walked through the door and stopped in amazement. Instead of the stone walls and ceiling and bare ground that she expected, she found that she was looking at a beautifully decorated, brightly lit room, with rich tapestries hanging down along the walls, and a lovely thick carpet on the floor. At one end of the room, a huge fire crackled in the grate, and there were two old-fashioned low stools with rounded seats on either side of it.

'But... from the outside,' she began.

Rhian smiled. 'It's magic,' was all she would say. 'Would you like something to eat or drink?' the Woman of the Isle then asked.

'No, no.' Louisa shook her head. Her grandfather had told her never to eat or drink any of the food of fairy land. He had told her stories about boys and girls who had done so and had then been trapped there for years because of it. 'I must go now,' she said, 'it's getting very late.'

Rhian bowed and stood back, allowing Louisa to hurry outside onto the island. Night had fallen and the stars were hard and sharp in the purple-black sky.

'Well, I'd better be getting home,' she said, 'my parents will be wondering what has happened to me.'

'Of course,' the Woman of the Isle said. She raised her long-fingered hand and touched Louisa's shoulder. 'Before you go... is there anything you would like to say to me?' There was a strange look in her eyes as she asked, and her voice sounded strained.

'I don't understand,' Louisa said. 'Except, of course, thank you, you have been very kind.'

Rhian smiled sadly. 'Is there nothing else?'

Louisa backed away towards the beach. 'Well... thank you again.'

'Is there nothing more you can say to me?' Rhian asked, and her eyes were damp with tears.

The girl began to get a little frightened now. She shook her head. 'I've already said thank you,' she said. 'What more can I say?' And then she jumped from the floating island onto the beach. She turned and ran up the beach to the foot of the tall, dark cliffs, the stones rattling under her feet.

And when she looked back the island was gone.

Louisa hurried up the path to her house. There was a light burning in the window and the front door was open. She could see the shape of her father standing in the door, with her grandfather behind him.

'Where have you been?' her father demanded. 'Do you know what time it is? We've been worried sick.'

'I'm sorry,' she panted. 'But wait until I tell you what happened...'

Louisa told her story to her father, mother, brothers and grandfather as they sat around the kitchen table drinking hot tea. Her brothers laughed and thought it was all a great joke, but neither her parents nor grandfather said anything, and in the end her mother sent her brothers to bed because they would not behave themselves. When they had gone, her grandfather asked, 'And did this lady ask you anything as you left the island?'

Louisa looked at him strangely. 'Yes, how do you know?'

Her grandfather shook his head. 'Tell me what you said first.'

'I thanked her for her kindness,' she said.

'And that's all?'

The girl nodded and yawned. 'That's all. Why?' she asked.

Her grandfather smiled a sad little smile. 'That woman was your grandmother,' he said. 'I first met her over sixty years ago, on a night such as this. I didn't realise then that she was of the fairy folk and I fell in love with her. I stayed with her for three nights and when the time came for me to leave she asked me that question. Like you, I just thanked her. What I didn't know was that if I had said *"God Bless You"*, the island would have remained stuck to the shore, and she could have come onto the beach.' He smiled sadly again. 'She appears once in every seven years, looking for someone to say those three words, so that she will be able to come looking for me...'

'I didn't know, grandfather,' Louisa said sadly.

The old man smiled. 'Of course not. And sure, she'll be back in seven years' time. I might meet her then...'

But the floating isle still appears off the west coast of Erin, and the Woman of the Isle is still waiting for someone to say those three simple words, 'God Bless You'.

CHAPTER TEN

The Sunken Town

Bannow lies on Ireland's south coast in the county of Wexford. It was once the site of a large mining town, but nearly all traces of the town have now gone, buried beneath the ground. All that remains now is a ruined church and some gravestones. The spot is known as the site of the Lost City of Bannow, and it is still possible to visit it . . .

Donal propped his bike against the stone wall and waited for his cousins to catch up with him. They were not used to cycling and had been slowly falling behind over the last few hundred yards. He looked back; he could just see them coming up over the hill.

He leaned on the wall and stared out over the sandy hillocks towards the sea. Before him was the small overgrown graveyard and behind that the ruins of St Mary's Church. It was all that was left of what had once been the large town of Bannow.

There was a squeal of brakes behind him, and he turned around as his three cousins climbed off their bikes and flopped to the ground, red-faced and panting.

'*Wow*! You didn't tell us it was so far,' Paul, one of the boys, said.

'It's not,' Donal said, laughing. He was the oldest of the four, having just turned twelve. He had short coal-black hair, black button eyes that always seemed to be laughing, and an Irish sense of humour. 'It can't be more than six miles.'

'Six miles!' Susan exclaimed. 'But that means another six miles back.' Susan was eleven, two years older than her twin brothers, Paul and Simon. The three cousins came from London, but were spending part of their summer holiday in the south of Ireland with their aunt and uncle. She looked up at Donal. 'That's twelve miles!' she sighed, shaking her head from side to side, her long blonde hair catching in the slight breeze.

'It's not that far,' Donal said, with a smile, 'and in any case, it's worth it.'

'I hope so,' Simon said, pulling off his shoe and examining a blister on his heel. His twin, Paul, came over and showed him a blister on the palm of his hand. They were almost identical except that Simon, who was two minutes older than his brother, as he kept telling people, had slightly darker hair. Their parents often joked that Paul's hair was the colour of fresh butter while Simon's was the colour of margarine. But Donal still had trouble telling them apart.

Susan stood up. 'Well, what have you brought us here for?' she asked.

Donal pointed down towards the ruins. 'That,' he said.

'That!' Susan almost shouted. 'A graveyard and an old church. We have those back home in England,' she said.

Donal climbed up onto the wall and hopped down into the field behind it. 'Ah, but do you have any buried towns?' he asked.

The twins looked up, suddenly interested. 'A buried town, where?'

'Down here,' Donal said. He reached up and helped Susan down into the field, while the twins scrambled up over the stone wall themselves.

'Where's the town?' Simon asked.

'Well, he did say it was buried,' Paul reminded him.

'Come on,' Donal said. 'I'll show you where it was.' He set off towards the church, with Susan beside him and the twins a little way behind. 'That's Bannow Bay,' Donal said, pointing off to the right. 'Over there is Fethard Bay, and beyond that, the Atlantic Ocean.'

Susan shaded her bright blue eyes against the glare of the sun on the water. 'What do the names mean in Irish?' she asked. During her holiday, she had become very interested in the names of places in the Irish language.

Donal thought for a few moments. 'Well Bannow Bay could mean Piglet's Bay,' he said slowly, 'and Fethard means the High Wood, I think.'

'Piglet Bay and the High Wood Bay,' Susan repeated. She shook her head. 'I think they sound better in Irish.'

They were now in amongst the graves, quite close to the ancient church. The twins wandered amongst the old gravestones, picking bits of moss and grass off them, trying to make out the dates.

Susan pointed to the church. 'What is it called?' she asked.

'It's called St Mary's Church,' Donal said.

'And when was it built?'

Donal shrugged. 'Some time in the thirteenth century,' he said. He pulled his jumper over his head and tied it around his waist by the sleeves. 'Come on, I'll show you the town.'

There was very little to see. There were long straight lines in the ground that marked the walls of houses and the edges of streets. Here and there stones broke through the surface of the earth, and there was a short square piece of stone stuck up from under the ground a little way, which Donal said was part of a chimney of a house buried far beneath the surface.

'What happened to the town?' Simon asked, after a while.

'The soil around here is very sandy and loose,' his cousin replied, 'and over the years the sand built up against the sides of the houses, and then began to cover them. When it began to block off the roads, the people thought it was time to leave.'

'Oh, I thought it had happened in a single night – like Atlantis,' Paul said.

'Or Pomp... Pomp... Pompeii,' Simon added.

'Oh no, this happened over a number of years, many years in fact,' Donal said. 'But in ancient times it was a very famous town, and the Danes had a mint here.'

'A mint?' Simon asked, 'what for?'

'For making coins, stupid,' his twin laughed.

'The High Street was here,' Donal said, pointing to a long grassy rise in the ground, 'and over there was Little Street and there was Lady Street.' He turned around to Susan. 'What do you think?'

'I think I'm hungry,' she said. She looked at her small gold wristwatch. 'It's nearly half past one.' She turned around to the twins. 'Go back to the bikes and get the food while Donal and I find some place to sit.'

'I know a good place,' her cousin said, and headed off around the side of the church.

The four cousins ate their lunch sitting on a broad, flat stone behind the old ruined church. The sun was now directly overhead and was reflected back off the old stones making all the children feel very warm and sleepy. When they were finished Donal stood up and stretched. 'Do you want to start back now?' he asked.

Susan yawned. 'In a few minutes,' she said, leaning back on the warm stone and picking an apple out of the basket. She closed her eyes and began to eat it slowly.

Donal nodded. He sat down again and rested his chin on his knees and stared out over the sparkling waters of the bay, watching the sea-birds rising and dipping slowly and then suddenly swooping into the water after some unlucky fish.

The two twins wandered around the ruined church for a little while, but soon they too grew tired and came back to the warm stones to lie down and rest before the long cycle back home.

A little while later, they were all asleep.

Donal awoke first. He sat up slowly and rubbed his neck, which was stiff and sore from the position in which he had fallen asleep. He looked around. Susan was stretched out on the stone beside him, fast asleep with her mouth open, snoring very daintily. A half-eaten apple lay on the ground beside her, where it was being slowly picked over by a long string of ants. The twins had fallen asleep in each other's arms in the soft bracken that grew close to the walls of the ruined church. Donal smiled; asleep they looked even more alike.

He glanced at his wrist, but then remembered that he had left his watch at home. He sat up and twisted his head to look at Susan's tiny gold watch.

Half past four!

Donal got a fright then; they must have been asleep for over two hours. He rubbed his arms which, although they were already brown from the sun, were sore. Susan's arms, legs and face were bright red from sunburn. The twins weren't so bad because they had been sheltered by the walls of the church, but he decided he had better take them home quickly. His mother had a special cure for sunburn which she made from milk and herbs.

Donal was just about to lean over and shake Susan awake when he saw movement out in the graveyard. It was just a flash of red and then it was gone. Donal froze, his heart beginning to beat quickly. Bannow was a lonely spot and usually when he came here there was no one around. He stayed very still.

He caught the flash of movement out of the corner of his eye again, and he had the impression of red and green and brown ... and a shape – almost man-like.

And it was coming closer.

Susan stirred in her sleep and opened her eyes. She raised her hand to shade her face from the sun, but Donal quickly leaned over and pressed his hand over her mouth. He put his own mouth close to her ear, and whispered softly, 'Don't say a word, don't even breathe, there's something moving out in the graveyard.'

Susan struggled to sit up, but Donal pressed her back down against the flat stone. 'Don't move,' he whispered softly, 'we're sheltered here, we can't be seen.'

The shape continued to approach the church, dodging and weaving through the gravestones, appearing for a moment and then disappearing almost into the ground. Donal squinted against the sun's glare, trying to make out the shape – although he already had an idea what it might be...

Suddenly the figure disappeared... and then it hopped up onto the stones directly in front of the four children!

Donal shouted with fright and Susan screamed, waking the twins. They both began to cry with fright. However, the small figure also got a fright. It balanced on the stones for a moment, its two arms waving about and then fell off – right at Donal's feet!

It was a small, red-faced man no bigger than the twins, wearing a bright green coat and a red cap, and a pair of large silver-buckled black shoes.

'It's a cluricaun!' Donal gasped.

'A what?' Susan whispered, moving as far away from the small man as possible.

However, once he got over his fright the cluricaun got up and dusted himself off. He then took off his cap and bowed deeply to the girl. 'He means a leprechaun, young lady,' he said in a high-pitched, almost musical voice. He then bowed to the twins and finally to Donal. 'I am Donn Dearg,' he said, 'Red Donn my friends call me.'

Donal smiled with relief. He knew there was no harm in leprechauns, unless you harmed them or tried to cheat them in some way. 'My name is Donal...' he began.

The leprechaun nodded. 'Yes, I've seen you here before,' he said.

'And these are my cousins, from London,' Donal added.

'In England,' Susan said.

'My lady,' the leprechaun said swiftly. 'I have relatives in London, England, and also in Glasgow,

Scotland,' he added with a grin.

'I'm sorry, I didn't think an Irish leprechaun would know about London,' she said.

'But I belong to the Fairy Host,' the leprechaun said, 'all the leprechauns, cluricauns, fir bolg, fir dearg, banshee, Shining Ones, and Phooka of Ireland are related to the English Hyther Sprites, Pillywiggins, Tiddy Ones, Vairies and Feeorin as well as to the Scottish Light and Dark Fairies and Elves and the ferocious Red Caps. I also have relatives in Wales among the Tylwyth Teg, the Sleigh Beggey and the Bendith y Maumau.'

When he paused for breath, Donal took the opportunity to speak. 'This is Susan, and these are the twins, Simon and Paul.'

Don Dearg looked closely at the twins. 'In my time twins were thought to be very special people,' he said.

'We are!' Simon said quickly.

'Ah, but can you do magic, ride the wind, or raise storms or bring rain? No? But that's what I meant about being special.'

'What are you doing here?' Susan asked. 'Do you live here?'

The leprechaun suddenly grew very cautious. 'I live around here,' he said, and then added, 'a lot of the *Daoine Sidhe* live around here.'

'Why?' Donal asked.

'Because it's a very special place. It's very ancient; there was a fairy fort here long before the town of Bannow was built.'

'What happened to the town?' Donal asked.

The leprechaun turned his back on the children and looked out over the low mounds and ridges which marked the old town walls. He shook his head slowly. 'I can remember when this was a rich, flourishing town, and before that I can remember the rich pasturelands, and before that I can remember the old De Danann fort that used to be here. But that was a long time ago,' he said, turning back.

'Tell us what happened,' Susan begged, and the twins said, 'Yes, please do.'

Donn Dearg hesitated for a few moments and then he sat down on the stones beside them. 'I can only stay a few minutes,' he said, 'but I'll try.' The small wizened man pulled out a long white pipe and quickly filled it with a fine green tobacco. He whispered a word and touched the end of his finger to the bowl and immediately began to puff thick clouds of smoke.

'How did you do that?' Simon asked in a whisper.

Donn Dearg smiled and winked. 'Magic,' he said, and began his tale. 'The town of Bannow was built on the site of a fairy fort. Now, while the *Daoine Sidhe* didn't like this there was little they could do without drawing attention to themselves – and the fairy folk do not like to draw attention to themselves. So they held a great council and decided that if the Human Folk did nothing to disturb them, they would leave them in peace.

'And so they did for a while.

'But then the Human Folk discovered that there was precious metal in the ground around their town, and so they began to dig down into the earth. Well, the *Sidhe* couldn't allow that now, could they?' Donn Dearg asked.

'Why not?' Susan wondered.

'Why not? Because they live in the ground, little lady, and how would you like some giant digging a great big hole in the roof of your house?'

The twins giggled at the thought of a giant

digging a hole in the roof of their house in Chelsea, but Donn Dearg shook his head. 'It's not funny, you know.'

Donal shushed them. 'Go on,' he said to the leprechaun.

'Well...' said Donn Dearg, and puffed angrily on his pipe, sending clouds of white smoke up into the clear blue sky. 'Well, all the fairy folk gathered together on the beach down there, and, with the help of some of the Sea-Folk, they worked a piece of the Old Magic.'

'What's Old Magic?' Simon asked.

'The most powerful kind in the world,' Donn Dearg said. 'Anyway, they worked some of the Old Magic and from that night onwards the fairy folk have been slowly covering the town with sand, burying it deeper and deeper. In a few hundred years there will be nothing left, nothing at all.'

'I wonder what it looked like,' Susan said quietly, looking out over the ruins.

Donn Dearg smiled sadly. 'It was nice,' he admitted. 'I liked it. In the morning with the sun shining on the white-washed houses it looked lovely, and in the evening, with the sun turning the thatch to gold, it was really beautiful.'

'I wish I could have seen it,' she said.

Donn Dearg looked over at her. 'Do you really?' he asked.

Susan nodded.

He looked at each of the children in turn. 'Would you like to know what the town looked like?' The three boys nodded. 'All right then,' the leprechaun said. 'Take hold of each other's hands,' he ordered them, and then he took hold of Susan's hand in one of his and Donal's in the other. The twins were holding each other's hands and Paul was holding tightly onto Susan's other hand. 'Now close your eyes,' Donn Dearg said.

'What are you going to do?' Donal asked, alarmed now. He knew enough about the fairy folk to know that they sometimes took children away with them.

'I'm going to show you Bannow from the very beginning,' Donn Dearg said. 'Now, close your eyes.'

Donal squeezed his eyes shut. He felt a cold breeze blow across his skin and ruffle his hair – although there was very little breeze that day – and then he felt the air change from warm and dry to warm and wet.

'You can open your eyes now,' Donn Dearg said. 'But keep holding hands – don't let go.'

The four children opened their eyes ... and found that the ruined church and the graveyard had disappeared. Everything had changed. There were trees everywhere, tall, thin trees that stretched up into the heavens, and short broad, wide-bodied trees that looked very, very old. There were holly bushes growing around most of the trees and, instead of the sandy soil, the ground was covered with lush green grass.

There was movement amongst the trees, and then strange riders on tall, thin horses rode into the small clearing. They were wearing long grey cloaks that shimmered with the damp dew and beneath their cloaks they wore silver armour and carried swords and spears of silver. They stopped and looked around, and seemed to look right through the children and the leprechaun. More riders arrived and there were small, dark men with them that looked very like the leprechaun. The taller folk then gathered around in a huge circle, joined hands and bowed their heads.

A blue spark suddenly danced around them and then it shot out and touched the trees and bushes, turning them to dust. In a few heartbeats there was a huge clearing in the centre of the forest, with nothing but a pile of grey dust to show where the trees had once stood. Even as the children watched the dust shifted and scattered on the breeze.

More riders arrived, bringing supplies in broad big-wheeled wagons pulled by oxen. These brought stones, polished white, black and green marble, smooth slates and shales and glittering quartz. Soon a palace began to rise in the clearing. The *Sidhe* folk used their magic to build a tall, strong fort of marble, roof it with slate and shale and use the quartz for the windows.

Time must be passing very quickly, because the four children could see the clouds racing across the sky, like a film speeded up, and they saw a wall growing almost magically around the fort. Then more riders came – but these were not like the ones they had seen at first. These were demon folk, looking like huge snakes and each one only had a single leg, riding demon horses that looked like dragons. There was a battle, and the demons were beaten back. Again they came and again they were beaten back. The children saw the blue-white magic of the *Sidhe* battle against the red-black power of the demons. But the blue-white magic was stronger and the demon folk were defeated forever.

Once again time slipped past very quickly, and the cousins saw that there were fewer trees now and they could see the blue of the sea sparkling in the distance. There were new invaders now and these were the most powerful of all, because these were men and they brought with them a most fearsome weapon – iron. And the *Sidhe* folk had no protection

against the iron swords and spears of the men.

So the *Sidhe* folk left the world of men and went to their Secret Places, the hidden forts beneath the ground, the floating islands in the sea, the Land Beneath the Waves, and the lost valleys.

Years slipped away quickly and the children saw the fairy fort begin to crumble. First a few slates fell from the roof, and then one of the windows fell out, and soon the great gate cracked and slipped from one hinge. Grass and weeds soon took over and then more and more quickly the walls began to crumble and fall to the ground, until eventually – although it must have been many, many years later – the fort was nothing more than a tumbled pile of stones.

And then the fairy folk came back. There were only a few of them; two of them were tall and very beautiful – a man and a woman, and others of them were smaller, darker people – the Earth Folk. The Earth Folk moved about quickly, shifting some of the stones and digging down deep into the earth, and then the Sidhe used their magic on the small hill. The ground heaved up and glowed a bright eerie green, and then a door opened in the grass and the children found that they could see down, far down into the earth. More and more of the *Sidhe* folk came then and went down into the earth. Then the door disappeared, leaving no trace of it behind.

Time passed quickly again. Now a lot more of the trees had disappeared and the cousins could see the sea quite clearly. They found that there were ships in the harbour, tall square-sailed ships with many oars – and with a dragon-shape carved at one end. These were the Vikings. They had just started raiding the coasts of Ireland, robbing the towns and taking prisoners to sell as slaves, but now more and more of them were settling in small towns close by the sea. The Vikings built a town quite close to the fairy fort, a rough town of wood and stone buildings, surrounded by a tall wooden fence with sharpened spikes.

Soon this town gradually disappeared and was replaced by a more permanent one of stone. The new invaders began to dig into the ground and began to mine a dull silver-grey metal from the earth. The metal was brought to a tall building in the town which seemed to be puffing out smoke day and night up into the sky, and every now and again, men would carry out boxes from this building, put them into the back of carts and ride away with them.

The town grew and grew, and then some workmen arrived with a small dark-skinned man in a rough brown robe. He seemed to be pointing directly towards the children, but the workmen just nodded and came over and started to dig. Very soon a building began to grow up beside the children. It was the church. The graveyard came next and soon spread out all around them. Bannow was now a large prosperous town, with many stone houses, and larger buildings in it.

The mines continued, and quickly spread further and further out around the town, and very soon they approached the site of the ancient fairy fort. Some of the men seemed to be objecting to digging near the mound, but others just ignored them and continued, and began to dig into the side of the fort.

In the blink of an eye the children found that a whole day had passed and it was now night time. To one side they could see the lights of Bannow town and before them they could see the fire of the watchman as he guarded the newly dug pit in the fort. But what the cousins could also see was the opening appearing in the fort above his head and two of the tall, thin people coming out. They looked towards the town and raised their arms and seemed to be clapping their hands. They then turned and headed off to the shore.

The forest quickly came alive with rustlings and creakings. The children saw the shadowy figures of small men, tall people, ghostly horses, and others heading towards the beach. From where they were standing they could not see what was happening down there, but they saw the streamers of light that shot up into the heavens, darting and spinning, spitting golden sparks and silver streamers down onto the town – but strangely enough none of the townspeople seemed to notice.

Time slipped away again, and now the children found that there were no trees left and they could see the sea quite clearly – only it seemed to be different. Was it closer or further away? It was hard to tell. But then they noticed that everything was covered with a fine layer of dust, and as time speeded up again, they saw the dust drift in over the town, first creeping up along the walls, sifting in through the windows and then covering the roofs. They saw some of the roofs cracking beneath the weight and crash to the ground. They saw the crops dry up and die in the sandy soil and, even as they watched, they saw the houses disappear beneath the shifting sand. And when they were covered, grass began to sprout on top of them.

The church remained untouched because the fairy folk's curse had no power against it. But with no people to serve, it soon fell into disuse and then into disrepair, and it gradually crumbled away, leaving only a shell behind.

And now a fog seemed to come down, a thick, cold

damp fog that covered everything and made it impossible to see even the hand in front of your face. The air grew cold and damp – and then suddenly it was warm and dry and the fog vanished – and the four children found that they were back beside the old ruined church with the sun beating down on their heads.

Donn Dearg let go of Donal's and Susan's hands with a sigh. 'That is what happened,' he said sadly. 'The townspeople shouldn't have tried to dig into the fort – but they were greedy, and their greediness not only destroyed them, but also their town.'

Susan pressed her hands together and rubbed them hard. She found she was trembling just a little. 'It looked... it looked like it was a very lovely town,' she said.

Donn Dearg nodded. 'Aye, it was.' He stood up on a tall stone and pointed towards the ridges in the ground. 'High Street was there – Weaver Street over there. The Upper and Lower Streets crossed there, and behind them was St Tollocks Street and then St Mary's Street came right up to the church. Down there St Ivory Street ran into Lady Street...' He nodded again. 'It was a lovely town.'

The leprechaun hopped down off the wall and turned back to the four children. 'I must go now, but thank you for your time, and for being patient enough to listen.'

'No,' Donal said, 'we should be the ones to thank you!'

'Yes,' Susan agreed, 'I don't think we'll ever forget it.'

Donn Dearg bowed to each of the four children in turn and then turned and ran off amongst the gravestones, finally disappearing down behind the tumbled stones.

When he was gone Susan turned to Donal. 'Was he real? Were we dreaming?'

'If we were then we were all dreaming the same dream...' He looked around for the twins, but they had run off into the gravestones in the town, and seemed to be looking for something. 'Come on,' he shouted. 'We've a long way to go.' He turned and walked back towards the bicycles with Susan.

'You know no one is going to believe us,' she said.

'Don't tell anyone then,' he said.

'But people should know what happened here!' Susan insisted.

'We need proof,' Donal said. 'We need to be able to show them something from the old town.' He turned back and looked for the twins. 'Come on,' he shouted, 'hurry up.' He looked at Susan's watch. It was nearly five o'clock.

They climbed up onto the bikes and waited for the twins who were running through the graveyard towards them. 'It might have been a dream,' Susan said slowly. 'It's called a mass-hallucination.'

'A what?' Donal asked.

'A mass hallucination is when a group of people all think that they can see the same thing.'

Donal looked unbelieving, but just shook his head and said nothing.

The twins came running up then. They were red-faced and looked as if they were both about to burst.

'What's up with you two?' Donal asked.

'You remember that tall building Donn Dearg showed us...' Simon began.

'The place where the people brought the metal and then carried out those boxes later on...' Paul continued.

'And you said that there was a mint here,' Simon said.

'Where they made coins,' Paul put in.

Donal looked at Susan and then nodded in confusion.

'Well, we were looking to see if we could find that building,' Simon began.

'And we did,' Paul finished. 'It was over there.' He pointed back across the field.

'So?' Donal asked.

The boys opened their hands. They were each holding a small round ancient-looking piece of metal.

'What are they?' Susan asked.

Donal picked one up and rubbed some of the grass and dirt off it. Underneath there was a silver coin. He turned to Susan. 'People will have to believe us now!' he said in triumph.

Of course people didn't believe the four children. But they did have a hard time explaining away the two silver coins which the boys had found at the site of the mint, and it was even harder for them to explain how the children knew the names of all the old streets of Bannow ...

Long, long ago, on a certain Christmas Eve,
in a certain old-world village . . .

The magical movie for all ages,
starring Dudley Moore as Patch –
and Santa Claus as himself

. . . Claus the woodcutter and his wife Anya brave the snow and wind in their
sleigh to bring hand-made wooden toys to all the village girls and boys. But
this night, as the childless couple struggles from cottage to cottage, they are
lost in a blinding snowstorm. Their sturdy reindeer collapse from exhaustion.
As Claus tries to rouse them, Anya sinks into unconsciousness. Freezing,
Claus feels himself going under, giving up, falling asleep.

Abruptly, they are awakened. The North Star is shining brightly overhead.
There is no blizzard. There is only the glowing star, and a glittering, torch-lit
procession of elves who joyfully welcome Claus and Anya to the elf village.
For centuries the elves have eagerly awaited the arrival of Claus – the one
who will fulfill the prophecy and carry gifts to children all over the world . . .

NOW AVAILABLE IN SPHERE PAPERBACK:
SANTA CLAUS NOVEL
THE SANTA CLAUS STORYBOOK
with over 50 spectacular photographs from the film
FOUR READ ALOUD STORYBOOKS
full colour storybooks containing episodes from the film, for children
ages 3–7
FOUR COLOURING AND ACTIVITY BOOKS
filled with puzzles, things to make and do, pictures to colour – for
children ages 3–8
JUMBO COLOUR BOOK
a big, fat colouring book filled with scenes and characters from the
film

A selection of bestsellers from SPHERE

FICTION

TOUGH GUYS DON'T DANCE	Norman Mailer	£2.50	☐
FIRE IN THE ICE	Alan Scholefield	£2.25	☐
SOUVENIR	David Kaufelt	£2.50	☐
WHAT NIALL SAW	Brian Cullen	£1.25	☐
POSSESSIONS	Judith Michael	£2.95	☐

FILM & TV TIE-INS

MOG	Peter Tinniswood	£1.95	☐
LADY JANE	A. C. H. Smith	£1.95	☐
IF I WERE KING OF THE UNIVERSE	Danny Abelson	£1.50	☐
BEST FRIENDS	Jocelyn Stevenson	£1.50	☐

NON-FICTION

WEEK ENDING: THE CABINET LEAKS	Ian Brown and James Hendrie	£2.95	☐
THE POLITICS OF CONSENT	Francis Pym	£2.95	☐
THE SPHERE ILLUSTRATED HISTORY OF BRITAIN VOLUMES 1, 2 AND 3	Ed. Kenneth O. Morgan	£3.95 each	☐

All Sphere books are available at your local bookshop or newsagent, or can be ordered direct from the publisher. Just tick the titles you want and fill in the form below.

Name _____

Address _____

_____

Write to Sphere Books, Cash Sales Department, P.O. Box 11, Falmouth, Cornwall TR10 9EN.

Please enclose a cheque or postal order to the value of the cover price plus:

UK: 55p for the first book, 22p for the second book and 14p for each additional book ordered to a maximum charge of £1.75.

OVERSEAS: £1.00 for the first book plus 25p per copy for each additional book.

BFPO & EIRE: 55p for the first book, 22p for the second book plus 14p per copy for the next 7 books, thereafter 8p per book.

Sphere Books reserve the right to show new retail prices on covers which may differ from those previously advertised in the text or elsewhere, and to increase postal rates in accordance with the PO.